To All of My Family and Friends

Thank you for your encouragement and your patience when I was more the writer than a friend. Special thanks to Clare Vertocnik and Bob Proske for all of their help.

Cover Design by Charlain Vertocnik-Roberts

Chapter 1

It's 3:00 a.m. when Dr. Andrea Parker says good night to her colleagues and walks out of the E.R. After working a twelve hour shift, three days in a row, and then a shift and a half, Andrea is beat. She walks slowly into the parking lot and barely makes it to her parking space. She digs her keys out of her black, Coach purse and slips into her silver, Mercedes sedan. "Ahh," she sighs as she closes her eyes and leans her head back against the cold, black leather seat. After a couple of minutes of deep breathing, she unties her ponytail, and lets loose her long, blonde, curly hair. She runs her fingers through it and massages the spot where her ponytail has been the last 18 hours. She turns on the ignition and starts her short drive home.

Seattle is beautiful even when it is so dark out. There are so many buildings and houses of different styles, especially the newer ones that were built on Newman Drive. Each house has its own

design and Andrea still can't decide which of the houses she likes

the most. Occasionally, she would turn down that street and look at

each one of them, but tonight she just couldn't wait to hit the bed.

She passes up Newman Drive and makes a left onto the next street

over, Oak Lane. Three houses down, she pulls into the driveway,

waits for the garage to open, then pulls in and parks. She walks into

the house thinking, *home sweet home*, as she turns on the lights and

sets the keys down on the kitchen counter. Three years ago, she

found an all brick, two bedroom house only ten minutes away from

the hospital, and she thought *perfect, just perfect*. With her busy

schedule, she hasn't had time to really make it homey, but she did

remodel a couple of the rooms to her liking.

Her favorite part of the house is the kitchen. It is now

considerably large thanks to the kitchen remodeling she had done right away. Andrea's favorite hobby happens to be cooking, and now she has all the space that she needs. She spends more time in the kitchen than she does in any other part of the house. She notices a plate covered with foil on the counter.

"Bella is the best," she says as she uncovers the plate and eats a chocolate chip cookie that her neighbor made.

Next door, lives a nice, older, lady of whom Andrea is quite fond. She reminds her of her own Grandma Rose. Bella Floriano is originally from Italy. At age seventeen, she ran away from home and came to the United States. One day, when Andrea asked her why she ran away, Bella smiled and said, "So that I could marry the man of my dreams!" She ran away with the man that she was in love with because their parents wouldn't let them marry.

Even though her husband had died 15 years ago, Bella still hasn't

moved on to a new relationship with a man. Bella has long, grey hair

which she wears twisted up in a bun, and she has dark, sparkling

brown eyes. And with no children of her own, she has spoiled

Andrea. They both know how to keep themselves busy, and that is

just one of the many things that Andrea and Bella have in common.

Bella keeps herself busy by going to church, having game nights

with friends, gardening, and cooking. Andrea takes extra hours at

work and when she does have time off, she usually spends it in the

kitchen cooking. When she has a free day, they like to get together.

They would make dinner, cookies, have coffee, and talk. If Andrea

has a Sunday morning off, together they attend mass at St. Anthony

Church. Bella is one the closest friends whom she has ever had. She

trusts and loves Bella more than anything. Without Bella, her life would be too depressing.

Andrea walks over to where the cappuccino machine is set

and prepares the coffee. After a few minutes, with a cappuccino in

one hand and the plate of cookies in the other, she walks

over to the breakfast table near the kitchen and takes a seat. Coffee

has the opposite effect on Andrea. Instead of giving her energy and

revitalizing her, coffee relaxes her whole body and mind that even

after drinking that large cup of the cappuccino she is ready to pass

out. After having eaten another cookie, she puts her empty cup in the

sink and she drags her feet to the fireplace and grabs her favorite

picture off of the mantle. It's a picture of her family taken eight

years ago at her college graduation. It is a picture of her Mom, Dad,

brother Matt, and Andrea in her cap and gown. She was so happy in

that picture.

She grew up in a small town, just outside of Denver, called

Green Hill. Andrea was homecoming queen and valedictorian of her

high school class. She was pretty, popular, and smart. She went to

Colorado State University, and after graduating, she went on to the

Seattle Medical Institute. Six years later, she became exactly what

she wanted to be. She is now an M.D. and is working as the

emergency room on-call doctor at one of the best hospitals in Seattle.

She sighed. She turned thirty, three months ago, and she has spent a

great deal of time since then thinking about her life. Andrea loves

Seattle, she loves her job, she has Bella, and yet she considers

herself depressed. Something in her life is missing and she still

hasn't figured out what that is. She embraced the picture that she

was holding and closed her eyes. *I still miss you.*

Two years ago, her parents were on their way home from a

charity ball when a drunk driver hit their car head on. Her father and the driver of the other vehicle died on impact. Her mother lingered a week in the hospital before she died from a head injury. Andrea hasn't been home since the funeral. Andrea has locked away the idea of visiting her family home because she has so many happy memories of her life with her parents there. Now that they are gone, she has a hard time thinking about returning and opening up her heart to those memories.

Matt and his wife Julia have taken many trips to Seattle to see her. Then, once last year, Matt took her to a cabin that he bought on a lake in Colorado. That was the only time that she had come back to the state. Andrea loved it at the cabin. She and Matt spent a whole week there all by themselves and she enjoyed every minute of it. But she couldn't bring herself to go to the house. She just couldn't go back to the one place that gave her so much happiness, but now reminds her of her loss. She sets the picture back on the mantle and heads off to bed.

Once in bed, she tosses and turns as she thinks about how unhappy she is. She thought about the best and happiest four years of her life when she was at Colorado State. The first half of her freshman year wasn't all that great, but then she met Luke. After that, she couldn't have been happier. She never thought that a person could give her so much happiness. Then it was over, and she was busy with her studies at the Seattle Medical Institute. She still thought about him even after all these years. She missed being in love and she wanted more than anything to be with someone. She wanted to share her life with someone, but all of the men that she has dated just never measured up to Luke. Finally, at 5:00 o'clock in the morning, Andrea falls asleep and dreams of Luke.

The doorbell rings at 9:00 a.m. and startles her. She jumps

out of the bed frantically and puts on a robe. She figures that Bella

has an emergency, so she runs as fast as she can down the stairs and

opens the door wide.

"Are you Dr. Andrea Parker?" A short, bald man shows her

his identification and says, "My name is Captain Corrigan and I

work for the Green Hill, Colorado police department.

"Yes, I am, what can I do for you, Captain?"

"I need to talk to you about something that happened last

night, to your brother and his wife. May I come in?"

"Of course, are they all right?" She asks nervously and steps

aside so that he can enter the house. Captain Corrigan takes a

minute and looks around to see if he is being followed and

then goes in. Andrea leads him to the living room and he takes a seat

on her brown sofa, as Andrea sits on the one opposite him.

"Last night, your brother Matthew was shot and Julia went

missing."

"My God, is he all right?" Andrea begins to cry.

"He's alive and he's in ICU at the hospital. He is lucky the

bullet just missed his heart. He lost a lot of blood. He's in stable

condition, but he's in a coma. The neighbor said that she usually sits

on her front porch on lovely evenings like we had last night. She saw

them in their car turn into their drive way at 11 pm. At midnight, as

she was returning into the house, she heard a gunshot. She quickly

ran in and called 911. We made it there in a matter of minutes,

but Julia wasn't there. The reason that I am here, is because I believe

that you could be in a lot of danger, too. Besides Mr. and Mrs.

Parker, you are the only family left. I believe that Julia was kidnapped and I think that they will call you for ransom."

"Why do you think that Julia was kidnapped?" asks Andrea.

"There was a note on their bed that said 'I won't stop until I get what I want'," replies Captain Corrigan, "usually that's something a kidnapper would write."

"My God." Is all that she could manage to say, and Captain Corrigan continues.

"We have a lot to talk about. I have arranged for us to go back to Colorado today on a 2:00 p.m. flight. Do you think that you can be ready by then?" he asks her.

"Yes, I will be ready, but right now I need some coffee. Would you like a cup?"

"Sure, that would be great." He follows her as she goes to the kitchen and puts on a pot.

As she pours him a cup of coffee, he fills her in on some more of the details, and asks her questions about Matt, Julia, and herself. She was surprised by some of the questions he asked, especially about the relationship that Matt had with Julia. But she figures that in order to find out what happened, the police had to look into everything. She didn't care how personal the questions really were. Her family has nothing to hide. Then, she went upstairs, dressed, and packed a suitcase. While she was packing, she called the hospital and told them about the situation. She would take a month long leave, and that she would keep them updated. She brought the suitcase and a light jacket downstairs and dropped them next to the front door.

"I am going to go next door to let my neighbor know that I will be gone," Andrea said and headed out of the door with Corrigan right behind her.

"You don't have to go with me!" Andrea exclaims as she looks back at him. "I will be back in just a few minutes."

"I know you feel that way," replies Captain Corrigan. "but I came all this way because I feel that you are in danger. I am not going to leave you out of my sight!" Andrea rolls her eyes and walks up to Bella's house. At Bella's door, Andrea knocks a couple of times.

"Good morning Andrea! It's a little early for you to be out and about isn't it?" She looks at Andrea and then at the man next to her. "Is there something wrong?" Bella frowns.

"Yes, there is. Bella, I need to talk to you. Can we come in?"

Bella gestures for them to come in and they enter Bella's house. She leads them to the kitchen and they each take a seat at the table. Andrea makes the introductions, and right away

Bella asks,

"What's wrong, honey?" Bella grabs her hand, and Andrea
starts to cry.

"My brother was shot last night and his wife is missing.

Matt's in the hospital, and the Captain here thinks that I am in

danger, too. So we need to go to Colorado today. I don't know

how long I will be gone. I need to go see Matt. I hope he makes it."

Andrea sobs and Bella quickly hands her a tissue, and gives
her a hug.

"It will be all right, my dear, you just go and be with Matt.

He needs you now. I will take care of everything at the house. So

you don't need to worry about anything here, and know that I

am keeping all of you in my prayers. Even you, Captain." She looks

at him hoping that he really does take care of the scared girl, whom she considers her daughter, sitting in front her.

"Thank you, Bella." Andrea wipes her eyes and blows her nose.

"We need to go, Dr. Parker." Corrigan interrupts and everyone stands up. Bella leads them to the front door and opens it.

"You take care of yourself, Andrea, and make sure to call me with any news." Bella says and Andrea hugs her goodbye.

"I will. Bye, Bella, and thank you." Bella watches them leave and waves again to Andrea before she closes her door..

_____ * _____ * _____

It is the longest flight of her life. She thought about Matt and how wonderful his life has been. Matt is three years older than she.

He is 6 ft. tall, and has blond hair and blue eyes. Matt is

a computer whiz. At age nineteen, he invented a computer software

program that made him a millionaire. He met Julia at 25 and they

married shortly after. Julia is petite, beautiful, and of Italian descent.

She has long, brown hair and hazel eyes. She is one of the sweetest

women Andrea knows, after Bella. Julia's parents retired and

returned to their homeland, Italy. Julia is an only child who came

from a very wealthy family. She attended a fund raiser one night and

that was how she and Matt met. Matt is well known around the

world, and is an important person in the Green Hill community. He

and his wife, Julia, work with many charities. Giving to the

community is just one of the things that makes him such a great

person. He is the most caring, giving person that she knows. *So why?*

Why Matt and Julia? Why would anyone want to hurt

them? She contemplates and draws a blank.

They get off the plane and go to baggage claim. She has just one suitcase. It is red with black trim, so it's easy to spot. She grabs her bag off the conveyor, turns around and bumps into someone. She loses her balance, but strong hands grab her shoulders and steady her.

"I'm so sorry," she says without looking up and trembles under the grasp of those hands.

"Andie, are you okay?" Only one person she knew called her Andie. She looks up and freezes. She sees those dark, brown eyes; those same eyes that once made her melt. She's in such shock that she can't say a word.

"Andie!" he gives her a little shake. She swallows hard.

"L-l-uke?" she somehow manages to say as a stutter. She

met Luke when she was a freshman in college. She had woken up late one day and was running to her class when she tripped and fell. Luke saw her fall, and came over and helped her gather her things that were scattered all over the sidewalk. As soon as she looked into his eyes, she knew that he would be the one. She fell in love with him right away. He was tall, dark, and handsome. He wore a fisherman knit sweater, and a pair of blue jeans. His hair was dark brown and short. He had a great hard body, not too buff, but pure muscle. He was funny and caring. He made her feel as if she was the most beautiful woman in the world. He made her feel so cherished.

The rest of their college days were spent together, and they were the happiest years of her life. After graduation, Luke proposed and she turned him down. She couldn't get married until she was done with school. She wanted to be a doctor ever since she was 11 years old, and her Grandmother Rosa died from colon cancer. The

day before her grandmother passed, Andrea promised herself that

she would become a doctor, so that she could save people. Marrying

Luke would have deterred her from fulfilling her dream. Marrying

Luke meant no MED school in Seattle. So she said "no" and they

parted ways, and haven't seen each other since. She spent many days

and most nights thinking about him. She knew that she would never

meet anyone like Luke again. Deep down, she always measured up

all of the men she dated to Luke. He was her first true love. He was

the love of her life that she let get away. Saying no to him that night,

was the one decision that she always regretted.

Chapter 2

"I can't work this case, Cap" he said angrily, when he realized who the victim was and his relationship to his lost love, Andrea Parker.

"You are one of my best detectives, Luke. You followed up on the call and I need you on this case. One of the richest men in the world has just been shot, and it looks as if his wife has been kidnapped. You don't have a choice."

"But Cap, I know the family," he snaps back. "I can't take this damn case!"

"That's enough Luke! You don't have a choice. I will be flying to Seattle this morning to pick up the victim's sister, Dr. Parker, and plan on returning this afternoon. I am expecting you to pick us up at the airport." Luke stormed out of the office slamming the door.

Luke came from a middle class family. His mother was an English teacher and his father was a police officer. His father was killed in the line of duty when Luke was fifteen, and that is when he knew he wanted to follow in his father's footsteps. He paid his own way through college by making money as a server at a restaurant near the campus. His mother had a heart attack and died a few years ago. As soon as he looked into Andie's eyes when they first met as college freshmen, it was love at first sight. She was the one that made his heart quiver. She was the one that brought him happiness, at least, she did until the night that he proposed, and she said no. That was the worst night of his life, and he will never forget how crushed he felt. He had spent extra nights working so he could save up and buy her a nice engagement ring. Once he had the

ring, he rented a hotel room, had it decorated with rose petals, and

popped the question, and all she could say was "I'm sorry Luke, I

can't." He was shocked and devastated. The way that things were

between them, he never expected her to say no. He thought she loved

him as much as he loved her. *Man, what an idiot,* he thought. After

that night, he swore that he would never again give his heart to

anyone.

Everyone at the station called him the heartbreaker. He dated

and had his way with plenty of women after Andrea. But he never

looked at women the same way he used to look at Andrea. Luke has

his heart secured in a cage. Every woman he meets and dates tries to

reach into his heart, but he keeps it caged up not to feel the repeat of

the pain that he suffered from Andie. Luke made sure that he was the one that was breaking all the hearts. He made sure that no

woman would hurt him as much as Andrea had. Now he is ordered

to the airport to pick up the one person he never wanted or expected

to see, again.

_____ * _____ * _____

"Yes, Andie, it's me. I came to pick you and Cap up. We are

going to drop him off at the station, and then I am going to take you

to the hospital to see Matt."

Captain senses Luke's frustration and interrupts.

"Detective Kith is the best detective in the city. I have

assigned him to the case. I sense that you two already know each

other." Corrigan smiles at her. "I hope that the two of you can put the past behind you and work together to help us find the people who have perpetrated this crime."

Andrea finally takes her eyes off of Luke and turns toward Captain Corrigan.

"Yes, we do know each other, I am just a little surprised to see him, that's all. Working with Luke will not be a problem." *Yeah right*, she thought to herself. She hopes there won't be a problem.

Luke grabs her bag and they head out to the parking lot. The ride to the station is horrible. She sat in the back and listened to the two of them talk about the case. She was shocked twice in the last 12 hrs. She never expected her brother to have been shot, and she sure didn't expect to see Luke. She only saw him in her dreams. He hasn't changed much over the last eight years. He is still as tall and muscular as she remembered him to be. His brown hair still looks messy, and sexy. She wonders if his hair still feels the same way, too. It looks like he hasn't shaved in a couple of days, as he is sporting a stubble that makes him seem a little bit older, and a lot more masculine. She stares at him from the back seat. He looks angry and tired. He looks as if he hasn't slept much. She thought about the one night that changed everything, and she shudders.

"You cold?" He asks her as he looks back at her from the driver's seat. He must have seen her shudder in the rearview mirror.

"No, I'm fine," is all she could say without looking at him.

"Dr. Parker, may I please have your cell phone? We want to add a recording device to it, in anticipation of the ransom call." Andrea hands the Captain her phone.

Luke pulled up to the station and Captain Corrigan steps out of the car. He walks over to Luke's side and rests his arms on the window.

"Make sure you take Dr. Parker where she needs to go. I will send Joe to you after your shift. Until then, you need to watch her. We can't take any chances. Just wait here while I have the tech men add a chip to her phone." Corrigan orders Luke.

"Yes sir!" Luke looks at him and rolls his eyes. Cap shakes his head at him, smiles and walks away.

"You can move up to the front now, Andie. I won't bite, I promise."

Andrea got out of the car, and took the seat in the front.

"I'm really sorry about your brother," he says. "I talked with Dr. Newman this morning, and she told me that she thinks that he will come to soon. She thinks that Matt will be just fine."

"Thank you," Andrea replies as she looks out the window.

"I take it that Cap has filled you in on what happened last night and you just heard what we followed up with today."

"Yes, he told me that he thinks that Julia might have been kidnapped, and that he thinks that I, too, am in danger."

"The whole house was trashed when we got there last night. We first thought it was a robbery gone bad, but nothing seemed to have been taken. We found the note next to your brother and we know that whoever did this wants something from them. We just don't know what it might be. We figure that Julia was kidnapped and we are hoping that you will get a ransom call soon. When was the last time you spoke with your brother?"

"I talked to him last week."

"Did he sound okay? Did he mention or say anything to you that you might find as odd?"

"No, nothing out of the ordinary. We talked about my work. Matty wanted me to take a vacation and come home to see him and Julia. I told him that I would think about it like I always do. He told me that I should deal with my problems head on, and that it's been too long since I had been home. You know, I haven't been back home since my parents' funeral." Andie's eyes start to water, but she holds back the tears.

"Did he say anything else?"

"No, only that he will see me soon. I don't think this is the rendezvous he had in mind."

"When was the last time that you saw your brother and his wife?"

"The last time I saw Matty and Julia was about three months ago. They came to Seattle to see me. It was my birthday, and Matty was worried about me. They stayed about a week. We went

sightseeing, to museums, and to the movies. We had such a fun time

together." The thoughts brought a smile to her face.

One of the tech officers runs up to the car and hands Luke

Andrea's phone. Luke checks that Andrea has her seatbelt buckled

and they head off to the hospital. Luke parks his car in the

hospital garage and turns to Andrea,

"Here is your cell phone. We put a chip in it that will record

the conversations. But you have to make sure that you press this

button to start recording." He flips open the phone and shows her the

button. Afraid to touch him, she takes the phone out of his hand

making sure that there isn't any physical contact and puts it in her

purse.

"Matt is on the fourth floor. We can go straight up there with those elevators." He points to a corner of the garage. They get off the elevator, and Luke leads the way. He stops at room 421, where a police officer is sitting on a chair outside of the room.

"Any visitors?" Luke asks the officer as he gets up to greet them.

"Only the doctor and a couple of nurses came by. I have been checking their ID's before letting them in. I get off shift in one hour, and Spiky will take over then."

"Okay Junior, this is Dr. Parker, she is Matt's sister," he says and Junior shakes her hand.

"You ready to go in, Andrea? We will be right out here if you need anything."

"Thanks." She says and enters the room. She is stunned because she never expected to see Matt in this condition. She moves closer to the bed and looks at him. He is hooked up to an IV, and he is on a ventilator. She checks his chart and looks at all the vitals on the machines.

"Gosh, Matty," she says to him as she grabs his hand. She pulls a chair close to take a seat next to him. "Please don't leave me. I don't know what I would do without you. I need you."

She squeezes his hand and puts her head down on it. *Please don't take him away from me, God. I will do anything. Just let him be okay. I will even go to church every Sunday, just please let him live,* she pleads with God as her tears flow. The knock on the door startles her and she jumps up as it opens. She wipes the tears with her hand as a woman in a doctor's uniform approaches.

"Dr. Parker, my name is Dr. Newman, I performed the surgery on Mr. Parker." She shakes her hand. Dr. Newman is in her late fifties, and has short, dark, curly hair. She looks very tired. "Do you have any questions for me?" she asks Andrea.

"First of all, I would like to thank you for everything that you have done for my brother. I looked at the chart, and I know that all we have to do is wait."

"You know, Dr. Parker, I have had a lot of experience with this type of case. I firmly believe that he will be fine. The statistics show that eight out of ten people have made it after this surgery just fine. It usually takes at least 72 hrs. for them to come to. He seems to be doing just fine for the time being."

"Thank you for that," Andrea says. "I feel a lot better now that I have talked to you."

"I will be here for another couple of hours. I will check on him before I leave for the night. If you need anything, just let me know. You can stay here as long as you like," Dr. Newman says and leaves. Andrea takes a seat by Matt and just holds his hand. Another hour passes by and Luke enters the room.

"Do you want a ride to the hotel?" he asks her. "I am about to head out?"

"No thanks. I think that I will just stay here. I don't want to leave him here alone," Andrea replies.

"Okay, then let me introduce you to your personal body guard. He is to make sure that nothing happens to you. He will give you a ride to wherever you will be going.

"Spiky!" He calls, and a short man in uniform comes into the room. He must be in his forties. He has dark hair and a buzz cut. He seems to be in pretty good shape. "This is Officer Mark Ambrose, but we all call him Spiky," Luke says to Andrea. "I will get going. You two get acquainted. You know what to do, Spiky," he says and leaves without giving Andrea another look.

He turns on his car and sits there for a minute. *Man, Andie hasn't changed a bit. She is wearing a dark, grey dress shirt that was two buttons unbuttoned, and a black skirt that stopped right above her knees. She is still slim and that skirt she has on shows off all her curves. God, she looks good.* He had such a hard time trying not to stare at her today. Her hair is still long, curly, and blonde. He remembered strumming his fingers through it as he made love to her. He remembered those long slim legs wrapped around him. He remembered how it felt to have her soft hands caressing his back as he kept plunging into her. *Snap out of it Luke!* He shakes his head and opens his eyes. He has a case to solve first. He will not think about her in that way. He will not do what he did before. He will not let her crush him again. Andie never loved him. If she did she would have not said no, she would have married him. He

will work as fast as he can to solve this case, and then she will go

back to her great life in Seattle. He won't need to see her,

and luckily, Cap didn't assign him to be glued to her. *After all these*

years, she shows up back into my life. All that heartache he felt that

night she left him, came back. He is still hurt and angry. He will stay

as far away from her as possible . He will be just fine, he thought to

himself as he pulled out of the parking lot and drove off.

Chapter 3

At about 11:00 pm, before she left the hospital, Dr. Newman came in to check on Matt and saw no change. So near midnight, Andrea asked Officer Ambrose for a ride to the hotel. Captain Corrigan made reservations for her to stay at Holiday Inn, she wasn't allowed to go to the house, and she was glad. She wasn't ready to go there. The nurses told her that if he comes to, that they would call her right away. She left the phone numbers where she could be reached at the nurses' station.

It was too dark out for her to see the surroundings as they headed to the hotel, so she closed her eyes and tried to soak in everything that has happened within the last 24 hrs. Twenty minutes later, Officer Ambrose drove into the hotel parking lot and parked the car.

"We are here," he says as he turns to look at Andrea who just then opened her eyes. "I will get your bags and then we'll go in." Andrea gets out of the car and stretches. She was exhausted. They enter the hotel and Officer Ambrose checks them in and proceeds to lead her to her room. They stop at the door and he goes in first to check it out. Once he cleared it, he let her in.

"My room is right next to yours." He shows her the door that joins them. "The door will be unlocked, so if you need anything, just come and get me. What time in the morning shall we be ready to roll?"

"How about seven?"

"Perfect," he replies as he enters his room, and closes the door. Andrea walks over to the bed where her suitcase was and opens it up. She grabs her big, white t-shirt and heads to the bathroom where she takes a shower. At one a.m., she finally lays down in bed.

Seeing Luke today was quite a shock. She had dreamt about what it would be like to see him again. But in her fantasies, he let her in with opened arms. Today, when she saw him, and when she looked into his eyes, she saw pain and anger. He seemed to be quite uneasy with himself, she wondered if it was because of her or the case itself. *Did he still not forgive her? Did he understand why she had said no?* If only she could go back. Even after all these years she still loved him. She has never stopped. She had dated a little in Seattle, but no one really caught her fancy. No one made her melt inside. No one made her feel how Luke did when he looked at her. Her most recent conquest was Eric. He seemed a little too perfect.

Eric was sweet, generous, good looking, and kind, but he still wasn't

Luke. He was tall, had dark, brown hair and the lightest blue eyes

that she had ever seen. She dated Eric for about two months before

she broke it off. No one could measure up to Luke, and that's all she

did when she went out with men. She would go home after a date

and spend a good half hour comparing the man she went out with

that night, to Luke. She could never forget him. He even haunted her

in her dreams. She finally closes her eyes, and falls asleep.

She heard a loud thump and awakened. She looked at the

little clock on the nightstand. It was 2:30 a.m.. She heard loud voices

coming from the other room where Officer Ambrose was

staying. She quietly got up and went to stand by the door. She put

her ear against the door and listened.

"Where is she?" A man with a low, deep voice asked. "She

is supposed to be here."

Officer Ambrose says, "I'm not telling you!"

"Have it your way then," she heard the man saying and then a shot being fired. She grabs her cell phone out of her purse, runs into the bathroom. She locked the door, hid between the toilet and the shower stall and called 911.

"Calling all units. Calling all units! Shots being fired at the Holiday Inn on 9468 Pleasant Drive."

Luke hears the call on his radio.

"Shit! That's where Andie is." He jumps into his car and drives as fast as he can to get there. His adrenaline is pumping and his heart is beating so fast that he thought it was going to jump out of him. He is so worried that he starts to swear. *Jesus Christ, she better be safe and sound when I get there.* He parked his car behind two other squad cars, and quickly got out of it. He notices the ambulance

and starts to panic. He runs over to Cap who was directing a group

of officers.

"What happened?" Luke asks.

"We don't know yet. We just beat you by a couple of

minutes. Dr. Parker called 911. She heard a gunshot, Spikey might

be hurt. The phone was disconnected, and we don't know anything

else. I was just about to send the troops in." Captain Corrigan

continues to give out his plan on how they will be entering the hotel.

The police officers split up and go their separate ways. Some

of the officers go to the back of the hotel, while Luke, Captain

Corrigan, and a few others go in through the front. Others

were ordered to search the surrounding area.

While the rest of the officers continue to search the

downstairs, Luke heads upstairs with Officer Ryan, and a couple of other officers. They first went to the room where Spikey was supposed to be at. They walk in with their guns drawn and see Spikey lying on the floor. Luke points to the other door. The door was unlocked, so they entered and saw no one. Luke sees another door and heads for it. This door was locked. He kicks it open and goes in. He checks the shower stall, walks next to it, and yells out

"Don't move! This is the police!"

"Don't shoot!" she frantically cries out, and he realizes that it's Andie. He puts his gun in the holster and embraces her.

"Thank God you're here," she says to him. He holds her tight as she buries her head inhis neck and starts crying.

"Shhh.. It's okay," he consoles her. "You are fine, it's all gonna be fine." He takes in a deep breath to calm his own, rapidly beating heart, and breathes in the same intoxicating scent

that used to drive him crazy."Shh.." He gently strokes her back. "It's

okay, I'm here," he tells her in a soft voice to get her to calm down.

As soon as her breathing slows, he seats her on the bed and stands in

front of her.

"What happened, Andie? Tell me everything. I need all the

details, so don't leave anything out."

"I was sleeping, and I heard a loud thump," she sobs. "Then I

heard voices, coming out of Officer Ambrose's room. So I got up

and went to listen by the door." Captain Corrigan walked in and

stood next to Luke,

"Please continue, Dr. Parker," he tells her and she does.

"I heard a man ask Officer Ambrose 'where is she?' Officer

Ambrose told him that he didn't know, and that's when I heard the gunshot. I ran into the bathroom and called 911.She looked up at

Luke who was watching her like a hawk. He was studying her

words, her tone, and her actions. The more he listened and studied

her, the angrier he became.

"How come you didn't call the police right away? And why

did you hang up with the dispatch?" he asks her angrily.

"Why don't you tell us what happened next," Captain

Corrigan intrudes and gives Luke a look of disdain.

"While I was in the bathroom, a man came in. He grabbed

my phone away and shut it off. He told me that he is looking for a

flash drive. And that if I don't come up with it soon, he will kill me

too. And then he left."

"So they were looking for some kind of program, a flash

drive? Did you get a good look at the man? Did you recognize the

45

voice?" Captain Corrigan asks.

"No, he was wearing a mask and he was dressed all in black. He wasn't alone. There was another man with him. Is Officer Ambrose okay?" Andrea looks up at Captain Corrigan and waits for a reply. She couldn't bring herself to look up at Luke again. She knows by the look he gave her a minute ago, how angry he is.

"Spiky was shot in the head, unfortunately, he didn't make it," Captain Corrigan replied. "Do you know what kind of program these two men were looking for?"

"I have no idea. Matt never talked about his work with me." Cap nods and tells Luke to meet him in the next room.

"What now, Luke?" she asks him.

"I don't know. I'm going to go and talk to the Captain. Why don't you get yourself together, get dressed, and meet us in the hallway," he leaves the room.

She stands up and decides to go to the bathroom. *I wish that Matt would wake up. I wish I knew more about the work he does.* She splashes her face with warm water, than wipes it with a towel. She looks in the mirror and sees how disheveled she is. She brushes her hair and pulls it up in a ponytail and then heads out of the bathroom, slips into slacks and a sweater. She takes a few really deep breaths before she decides to head out of the bedroom and join them.

The next room is full of officers working so she decides to sit on a little chair in the corner of the room. As soon as she sat down, a group of officers went into her room, to process it.

Luke sees her sitting on the chair, walks over to her, and asks,

"How are you doing?"

"Okay, I guess. What do we do now?"

"Well, at least now we know that they are after some kind of computer program. Our lab techs took all of the computers from the house to the station after the first incident. They are going through them, and hopefully, they will have some sort of an idea as to what these guys are after. It doesn't seem like these guys will stop looking for it, and they are dangerous. Now that they know that you are here, I am going to need you to get your bags and come home with me. You aren't safe here."

"Luke, do you think that's a good idea? I don't want to intrude on you, and cause more problems." She looked at him and tried to figure out what he was thinking.

"Yeah, well, Cap made it quite clear that I am to watch over you. That is an order that I have to obey. You aren't safe here, and I am not sleeping on a crappy bed in some hotel room. Quite frankly, neither one of us has a better option right now. So whenever you are ready, we'll leave," he says in a gruff tone of voice. He is not happy with this at all. He doesn't want to be around her. He doesn't want to do something that he might regret later. He doesn't want to babysit. He wants to go out and investigate, and close this case.

She went back to her room and grabbed her suitcase and purse. She didn't even have time to unpack, so she was ready to go in no time. Captain Corrigan and Luke were waiting by the front door. Luke took her suitcase from her and leads the way out. Captain Corrigan got into his car and waited for them to leave before he followed them out of the hotel parking lot.

Chapter 4

She noticed in the car on the way over that he isn't wearing a

wedding band, so she assumes that he isn't married. She wonders if

he has a girlfriend and her stomach gets tied up in knots. Twenty

minutes later, they drive up to a house. His house is an all brick,

bungalow on Park Avenue. It is too dark for her to see the way it

looks from the outside. The inside, however, is exactly as she

expected. It doesn't have much furniture, and it is all in order. No

clutter anywhere. Luke was always organized and orderly. That was

one of the many things she loved about him. They both like order

and a lot of space. He showed her around and right away she

became fond of the kitchen. It isn't that big, but it has plenty of room

for her to do some serious cooking. He has an island in the middle of the kitchen and two stools. He showed her the livingroom next. The livingroom has two leather couches and a dark brown, wooden coffee table. He has a huge flat screen TV facing the couches. Next, he leads her upstairs to a room and sets her bag down on the bed.

"You can have this room. Mine is the next one over. The bathroom is through this door," he opens it to show her. "The bathroom joins both of our rooms, so we are going to have to share it." He looks at her and notices her tugging on her earlobe. *Damn, he thought, all I really want to do right now is bite and lick that earlobe. What I really want to do is grab her, throw her on the bed, and show her exactly what she has been missing out on.*

"I'm gonna head to bed," he says to her and leaves the room, as quickly as he can. This is going to be a lot tougher then he thought. Since Andrea let him use the bathroom first, he couldn't have been more grateful. He turned on the shower, took off his clothes, and jumped in. After taking a much needed cold shower, he went to bed. He tossed and turned. He couldn't stop thinking about her. *Why does she have such a great power over me? What is it about her that makes me so weak?* He has no idea. All he knows is that he can't stop thinking about her. He couldn't stop thinking about that slim body of hers, and how good that body used to feel, naked, lying under him. He couldn't stop thinking about those breasts and how they used to fit perfectly in his hands. "Ugh," he pulls the pillow over his face. He can't still love her, can he? He has to stop thinking about her. His top priority is finding Julia and the bad guys. The faster he does that, the faster she leaves, and the faster he can forget about her.

Finally, at 4 am, having let Luke use the bathroom first, she changes into her big T-shirt and plops into the bed. Andrea always sleeps in a t-shirt and underwear. At least she has for the last eight years of her life. She didn't waste her money on nighties and sexy underwear anymore. It was pointless for her to wear sexy lingerie since she didn't have a man to impress. Sex has not been in the picture. Her only lover had been Luke. When he held her in his arms today, she felt her body respond in ways that she forgot were possible. His warmth went through her whole body jolting all of her senses. Now she is sleeping in his guest room, right next to his bedroom, hoping he would come to her. Hoping deep down that he still loves her.

_____ * _____ * _____

It's been two days since Andrea had arrived. She has spent

her days at Matt's side in the hospital. Luke hasn't even gotten close

to finding Julia or the two perpetrators. He has been cautious around

her steeling his feelings. He leaves before she gets up and comes

home late after she has gone to bed. During the day, he has been

spending most of the time at the station. Delving into the lives of

Matt and Julia, they were re-interviewing acquaintances, friends, and

all the people on their contacts lists. After he leaves the station, he

headed out to the Parker residence to keep a look out. He keeps

hoping that at least one of the scumbags would come back

one more time. He takes a sip of coffee and stares out at the house.

They haven't found what they were looking for, and neither did we.

The tech crew found nothing of interest on either of the computers from the house. It would be so much easier if they had found the flash drive. At least then they would be able to negotiate, Luke thought. No one they talked with so far had given them any leads in regard to the assault on Matt. Matt definitely didn't talk about work with anyone. They haven't made any headway, and Luke is really aggravated. They didn't even leave any fingerprints, and that pissed him off. *These guys are smart, very smart. They have been laying low for the last couple of days. Maybe they gave up,* he thought. *There is no way that I am going stop searching for them, they killed Spikey, one of our own. We still haven't found Julia, and they still haven't called Andrea for a ransom.* Luke has never quit a case, and he doesn't plan on quitting on this one either. All he needs is one little clue, the missing piece to the puzzle. One piece that could solve the puzzle to the crime.

A picture of Julia Parker has been on the news every day since the incident. The police department received plenty of calls. They followed up on every tip. But they still couldn't track her down. The last call they received was from a waitress at The Garden's Restaurant. She called thinking that she saw Julia. She said that a woman was having dinner with a man, but she wasn't 100% sure that it was Julia. She did give a description of the man that was with the woman. She said that the woman didn't seem like she was in any sort of distress and that she seemed quite complacent. *If Julia was kidnapped, then why wasn't there a call for ransom?* Luke wondered. His initial thoughts were that Julia wanted Matt dead. *If Matt dies, I suppose Julia would have it all. Julia would own all of Matt's property, stocks, shares…everything. I guess*

I would need to bring up this delicate matter with Andie. Does she have any idea about Matt's estate? So far, we can't say that Julia is a suspect. Andrea though seems certain that the two of them weren't having any marital problems. But then, why has Julia disappeared? Is she working with these guys? It's 11:00 pm, and he's been sitting in his car in front of the Parker's residence for the last three hours. He hates doing stake outs, but there is nothing else he can do, but wait for something to happen. "Damn," he slams his hands on the steering wheel and decides to finally go home. *It's late, and Andie should be asleep.*

He carefully walks into his house, not wanting to make too much noise for fear that Andrea would wake up, and turns on the kitchen lights, and finds Andie sitting on a stool by the kitchen island. She was dressed in a long white t-shirt and he took a second to gather his thoughts.

"Christ," he mumbles to himself as he enters the kitchen. You should have had the lights on in here."

"I couldn't sleep," she says.

"I see," was his only reply. He walked to the refrigerator and grabbed a pop.

"Are you hungry? I made lasagna for dinner today," she smiles at him.

"You know what? That sounds really good. I can't remember the last time I ate a home cooked meal." He sat down on one of the stools, and after heating it up, she placed a piece of lasagna on a plate in front of him.

"Thanks," he smiled at her. He couldn't get his eyes off of her. He watched her every move and felt his groin grow by the minute. *Thank God she can't see my lower half now.*

"How is Matt?" he asked as she sat down on the stool opposite of him.

"He is still the same. I hope that he awakens from the coma soon. I have been spending most of the time with him at the hospital."

"Has Johnson been giving you a hard time?" Johnson has had the duty to safeguard Andie while Luke was at work. As soon as Luke comes home, Johnson takes off and goes home to get a break. He returns to Luke's house at 6:30 in the morning and that's when Luke goes to the station. They have another officer at the hospital who keeps an eye on everyone who goes into Matt's room.

"I love Officer Johnson! We had a nice discussion while he escorted me to the grocery store. He has got to be one of the nicest men I know. He is such a doll!" Andrea exclaims.

Luke nearly chokes as he chews his food.

"Are you sure that we are talking about the same man here? I have never heard Johnson described like that! Johnson is never nice!"

"He seems pretty nice to me!" Andrea replies, and Luke is thinking that he is going to have a little chat with Johnson in the morning. Andie sits across from Luke and watches him eat.

"Andie, this was great! It totally hit the spot," he says to her as he moves his plate to the side. Her cheeks turn pink and she smiles. Andrea has the prettiest smile. When she smiles his heart skips a beat. He hasn't seen that smile in years. That smile just made his heart ache for her even more.

"Thank you, I'm glad that you enjoyed it. I haven't seen you much the last couple of days. I was starting to think that you were avoiding me on purpose," she says nervously as she looks at him from across the island.

"I have been working on the case, trying to get some leads. But to tell you the truth, Andie, these guys left nothing behind. No fingerprints, not even a piece of hair we could try to trace. I was hoping that they would continue to search for the flash drive, but they haven't shown up at the house again. I'm sorry that it's taking so long. Usually by now, we would have gotten some kind of lead. But no one that we have talked to knows anything about what Matt was working on."

That smile she had on her face a minute ago has turned into a frown. *Good going, Luke,* he thinks to himself. *Why do I have to be such an ass?*

"I'm gonna go back to the house again in the morning, do you want to come with me?" he anxiously asks her.

"Yeah, maybe I can come up with something you guys missed," she replies and stands up. She walks over to him and grabs his plate. As she grabs the plate, he puts his hand on top of hers.

"Leave it," he says to her in that soft voice of his that makes her body come alive.

He put the plate down, grabbed her hands, and pulled her to him. Afraid she would run, he put one hand on her lower back, while the other one held her chin up so that she looked right into his eyes. They stood like that for a few seconds as his mouth hovered over hers. Then he kissed her. He kissed her hard. He kissed her as if his life depended on just this one kiss. And she kissed him back with all the passion that she has, and for all the years she has missed kissing him. He brings their bodies closer together and ...crash...a window

breaks again. Luke pulls her down under the island.

"Stay down," he commands and crawls away from her, to the

window in the living room.

What the hell was that? she thought. One minute she was

being kissed and the next minute she was being pushed to the floor.

She sat on the floor under the kitchen island and pulled her knees up

to her chin and swayed back and forth. After a couple of minutes,

which felt like a lifetime to her, she calls out to him.

"Luke, are you there?"

"Yeah," he said as he came back into the kitchen. "I'm here.

You okay?" he asked as he pulled her up to her feet.

"It was a drive by, they threw a brick in through the

livingroom window with a note attached to it. Why don't you go change and come back down. My guys are on their way."

She, still shocked, nods and runs up to the bedroom. She quickly puts on a pair of jeans and a shirt, and runs back downstairs. She finds him sitting on the couch waiting.

"What does the note say?" she asks as she takes a seat on the other couch.

He stands up and starts to pace back and forth. He put his hand on his head and rubs his hair. *Oh, oh*, she thinks. *Luke is really mad now.*

"What did the note say?" she repeated her question. He stopped his pacing and looked at her.

"The note says, 'We know where you are, and we want that flash drive.' That's all it says. They must think that you know where it is, and what is on the flash drive. Andie, do you know something that I don't know? Have you failed to tell me something about Matt's work? You say that you and Matt are close."

"We are as close as siblings can be, but I don't know anything about a flash drive, I swear. I told you everything I know. Matt never discussed his computer stuff with me. Everyone knows that I don't understand computers. I wouldn't lie to you, Luke."

"Yeah, well I'm sorry I don't believe that. You didn't have a problem lying to me before." he snapped at her.

"What are you talking about? I never lied to you about anything!" Her eyes start to water as she looks at him.

He looks at her with icy eyes and spits out, "you just did." He just ripped her heart out and squashed it. She never lied to him about anything. She thought that he knew that she was as honest as it gets.

"What do you mean by that?" she asks him angrily. "When

did I ever lie to you?" The sound of the sirens approaching disrupted them. He looks away from her and the police storm in. There must have been at least ten of them. They quickly began their job looking around, talking and taking notes. Two of them were trying to get fingerprints off of the brick and the note. *This was going to take forever*, Andrea thinks to herself. She goes to the kitchen and puts on a pot of coffee. While the coffee was brewing, she decided to call the hospital and check on Matt. She was there earlier today and his condition still hadn't changed. *Usually by now, they wake up.* She has no idea why Matt hasn't come out of the coma. *Matt seems to be content, he must feel so safe locked away in his coma world.*

"We will get all of this to the lab right away. We will let you know as soon as we get something," one of the men says to Luke, as they all pack up and get ready to leave. It's been over an hour. The window is patched up with plywood.

She is sitting on the stool in the kitchen, drinking coffee, when Luke comes in.

"I suggest you go to bed now. When you wake up, we are going to take a ride to the house and look around again. A window repairman will be here in the morning to replace the window, so don't panic if you hear noise early."

Without another look her way, he left her all alone. He slammed the door to his room and sat on the bed. *What in the hell was I thinking! I completely lost it! I kissed her!* He is so angry with himself. *I shouldn't have kissed those luscious, sexy, lips of hers, I was way out of line. Then to call her a liar!! Jesus Christ! I am not 22 years old anymore.* He curses at himself and throws a pillow against the wall. He shouldn't have let his emotions intervene with the investigation. No matter how much he wanted her, he shouldn't have touched her. No matter how bad she hurt him a long time ago, he shouldn't have said what he did. He was angrier with himself then he was with her. He's been on edge ever since he saw her at the airport. He is so frustrated and anxious that he doesn't know what to do with himself.

She put the coffee cup in the sink and shut off the coffee pot. She is so mad at him. She can't believe that he called her a liar. He sure knows exactly how to push her buttons.

Chapter 5

In the morning, after the window repairmen left, Andrea makes some eggs and pours them each a cup of coffee. Luke walks into the kitchen, takes a couple of bites out of the eggs and drinks some coffee. Neither one of them says a word. As soon as he sees Johnson pull up in the driveway, he got up and went outside. Andrea watched them through the window. They talk for a few minutes and Johnson leaves. When Luke came back into the kitchen, he sat back down and he silently finished his breakfast.

"You ready? I will be out in the car, waiting," he told her and walked out.

Great, he's going to ignore me. Andrea clears up his dishes and heads out of the house. She got into the car and put on her seatbelt.

"Can we stop at the hospital first? I want to check on Matt."

She looked at him and waited for a reply. He nodded and drove off.

He didn't say a word to her at all. Every time she opened her mouth

to say something he shushed her. The more he did that, the angrier

she became. He parked the car in the parking lot of the hospital.

Luke escorted her to the room, but stayed out in the hallway and

talked with the other police officer, while she went in to see Matt.

The first thing she did, was walk over to Matt and give him a

kiss on the forehead. She walked around the room and checked his

chart and all of the monitors. She pulled up a chair next to the bed

and sat down. Then she talked to him. She told him about everything

that happened last night. She even told him about Luke and how they

kissed. Then she said a couple of prayers wishing for Matt to break

through the coma. Every time she comes, Andrea reads him

a couple of articles out of a magazine she bought the other day. She hopes that he hears everything she is saying to him. As she starts to read the second article, Luke walks into the room.

"We need to get going, Andie. I'll be waiting outside."

"Okay, just give me one more minute." She fluffs his pillows and gives Matt a kiss on the cheek. "Love you, Matty," she whispers into his ear, "get well soon, please."

At the Parker residence, Luke cuts the yellow tape at the front door, and they enter the house. The house hasn't changed since she was last home two years ago. It is located at the end of the street and has two large evergreen trees in the front yard. It is a huge house, with a huge in-ground pool in the back yard. She loved to swim. When she was in high school, she hosted many parties at the house. That was probably why I was so popular back then, she smiles to herself as she looks out the window and into the backyard.

She looks a little to the left and sees that the tree house her dad built

for Matt, was still there. It appears that Matt left the house in the

tree. Andrea knew that Matt and Julia planned to have children of

their own. Unfortunately, Julia had two miscarriages since they have

been married, but Matt still has high hopes. Once, when she was

thirteen, Andrea snuck up there when Matt wasn't home to see what

captivated him there. She always wanted to know what he did up in

that tree rather than socializing with peers. What she found in there

was a desk and a laptop - nothing else. Such a nerd! She smiled at

the memory of how Matt was. She remembered that Matt had

problems making friends. There was only one guy that she

remembered that used to hang out with him. *Jerry! That's his name.*

I wonder if they still talk. She hasn't seen Jerry since her parents' funeral. Matt hasn't mentioned him since then either.

She moved away from the window in the kitchen that overlooks the backyard, and started to walk and look around. The house was a mess. There were papers all over the place. Furniture was thrown around everywhere. She headed up the stairs to her room. She stops at the door that is sealed off with the yellow caution tape, apprehensive about what she would see beyond the door, she sighs and walks to her bedroom at the end of the hall.

Matt and Julia moved into the house after they got married. Mom and dad were so pleased. There was plenty of room, and they couldn't wait to have grandchildren running around. It's too bad that they were unable to have any before her parents died. She looked at her old room and sighed. Other than the disarray of the break-in, Matt had not changed a thing in her room. The queen sized bed with a wooden mantle as the head board, still held the pictures in frames on it. On either side of the bed are nightstands with lamps on them, now knocked over. The room has its own private bathroom, which she has loved over the years. She began cleaning up the room, creating a semblance of order. She never thought that she would be back here under these circumstances. She lets the tears flow as she sits down on the edge of the bed. She looks down and on the floor next to her foot is picture in a frame. She bends down and grabs it. It was a picture of her and Luke. They spent a weekend camping in the mountains. He had his arm around her and they were smiling. She wondered why he called her a liar and she thinks about that kiss. That kiss that made her want more, so much more.

Luke starts to search the office and notices that Andie is nowhere around.

"Andie!" he calls out, as Andrea appears on the staircase.

"I'm here," she answers. "I was just checking out my old room. I didn't find anything in there." She walks over to him. "I guess that I will take a look in the library." She takes a few steps and walks in to the library room, while Luke goes back into Matt's office.

The library room is pretty big and the walls are lined with books and music CDs. There is a wooden coffee table in the middle of the room, and two black, leather chairs behind it. She has no idea what exactly she is looking for. She started to pick up the CDs that were all over the floor. She looked at each one as she put them back on the shelves. When she finished with the CDs, she started to pick up the books. Her cellphone rings and it startles her. *It's probably Bella*, she thinks to herself as she pulls it out of her jeans' pocket and

75

answers it.

"Hello?"

"Andrea Parker?" A man with a voice she has heard before asks her.

"Yes, who is this?" she manages to say as she becomes aware of that deep voice that she heard a few nights ago.

"I know you are at the house, and I need that flash drive." That voice gives her the chills and she shivers. "You don't know me, but I know all about you. Your brother designed a software program called A.S.V.P. It stands for anti-spyware-virus-program. He doesn't have it saved on his computer. Knowing your brother, he put the program on a flash drive and hid it well. Are you listening, Miss Parker?"

Luke hears her talking on the phone and walks out of the

office.

"Yes, I'm here," she says and gives Luke a glance. He can tell by the look on her face that something is wrong, so he walks over and stands right next to her. He takes out his phone and mouths to her to press the recording button. She understands and quickly presses it.

"Listen well, Miss Parker, this will not be repeated." She shudders.

"I'm listening, please continue."

"I need you to find the flash drive. You have one week to come up with it or I kill Julia. Do you understand?"

"I'd like to talk to Julia first." After a few seconds of silence, someone gets on the phone.

"Hello," she hears a woman say.

"Julia, is that you?" Andrea asks

."Yeeesss it's me. Where's Mattyyy?" Julia slurs her words

and sounds disoriented.

"Julia, are you alright? Did they drug you?"

"Uh, huh!" Julia starts to giggle and the man gets back on the

phone.

"You have one week, that's it."

"But how do I get in touch with you?"

"You don't. I will be in touch with you. You have one week."

He ends the call.

"What's going on, Andie? Who was that?" Luke asks her.

She rubs her hands together and he knows she's nervous and scared.

"It was one of the men. He wants me to find the flash drive.

He said if I don't come up with it in one week, that he is going to kill

78

Julia." Trembling, she sits on the couch. "He said that the program is called A.S.V.P. It's some kind of anti-virus software program. He said it should be on a flash drive."

"Did your brother mention this program to you?" he asks her as he sits down on the other chair right next to her.

"No, the one thing my brother never discussed with me was his work. I told you all of this already. Matty knows I don't like computers. He never talked to me about them and what he did. You have to believe me, Luke." She pleads with him. He grabs her hand and holds it.

"Relax, Andie, I believe you."

"Luke, it's someone who was really close to my brother. My brother didn't discuss his work with just anyone. He wouldn't just give out important information like this to someone he didn't know well."

"Okay, tell you what, we'll go to the station and go over the contacts one more time. Maybe a name will pop out at you."

It's a long shot, he thought, considering that they already talked with everyone on the list. He doesn't want Andie to know that he suspects that Julia has something to do with this, that she is somehow involved of the attack on Matt.

"Do you think that you might know this person?"

"No, I don't think I know him. His voice doesn't sound familiar to me. I haven't been home since my parents died. I have no idea who their friends are. Matt never mentioned anyone to me," she replies. "The man on the phone said that I don't know who he is. But it was the same man who was at the hotel a few nights ago." She shivers again just thinking about the incident. He let go of her hand

and got off the chair. He places a phone call as he walks back into the office.

"Andrea got a call a few minutes ago. We are going to come down, maybe we can get the number off her cell, and link it to someone."

"That's good, I have some news and you will hear all about it when you come in." Captain Corrigan says and hangs up.

"Andie," he calls out as she steps into the office. "We are going to run down to the station. Make sure you bring your phone. We are going to need it."

_____ * _____ * _____

Now at the station, Luke leads her into a little office and

offers her a seat.

"Someone is going to come in here and talk to you."

"Talk to me about what?" she asks as she tugs on her ear lobe. He grabs her hand from her ear and sets it down in her lap.

"Relax, the officer will just ask you what was said on the phone, and then she's going to give you some pictures to look through. Your job is to look through them and see if maybe, someone looks familiar to you. I am going to take your phone down to the lab. When they are done using it, I will return it to you and then we'll be free to go."

"Do I have to sit here? I told you that I really don't think I know him. I really didn't see either of them that night."

"Yup, sorry," he replied and walked out of the room.

A few minutes later, a woman, with a stack of folders with

pictures in them enters. She sets all the files on the table in front of Andrea.

"My name is Officer Baily," she says as she holds out her hand and Andrea shakes it. She is in her thirties, tall, and slender. She has brown eyes, and her brown hair is up in a ponytail. She has great olive toned skin, and she has on just a little bit of make-up. She is beautiful. She has on a black suit with a white dress shirt under it, and her badge is pinned to her belt loop. Officer Baily sits across from her and spreads out all of the files.

"I am going to leave these here for you to look at. Maybe you will recognize someone in here. I am going to get a cup of coffee, would you like one?"

"That would be great, thank you," Andrea looks at her and smiles.

"You take cream and sugar?" Baily asks.

"Yes, please, I need a lot of cream and a lot of sugar,"

Andrea replies as Officer Baily heads out of the office.

The office is a little cubicle surrounded by glass. Andrea is

able to see everything going on outside of the room. She is glad that

she isn't all closed up. Even though she is by herself, she didn't feel

isolated from everyone else in the station. She starts to go through

the pictures, and after a few minutes, Officer Baily returns with her

coffee and even more files.

"Thank you," Andrea says as she takes the coffee from her.

"Did anyone catch your eye yet?"

"No, not yet."

"Well, you keep looking, I will be back in a few minutes to

check in with you. When I come back, I would like to go over the phone call. Or better yet, here's a pen and a piece of paper. Why don't you take a minute and write down the full conversation that you had on the phone. Make sure that you date it and sign it."

Andrea took the paper and the pen and started writing.

Officer Baily sits on one of the chairs and waits. Baily knows that the lab has a recording of the phone call, yet she felt compelled to make Andrea suffer a little. She can tell that Luke has feelings for this girl just because of his behavior the last few days. She noticed how Luke looked at Dr. Parker. She has never seen him look at another woman that same way. She asked him when she saw him at the office, why he has been acting so differently towards her. His answer was, *"I told you, Baily, that our relationship is strictly platonic. I told you when we first went out that I am not looking for a long term relationship."* Baily rolls her eyes. She has been in love with Luke since she started to work in Colorado a little over a year

ago. They went out many times, but Luke didn't want a relationship

with her. She still has hope though, but now she needs to get Andrea

out of the picture. She has been working on the case too, thinking

that they will solve the case faster. Andrea interrupts Baily's

thoughts by putting the pen down on the table. Andrea hands the

paper back to Officer Baily.

"All done." She smiles as Baily tugs it out of her hand. Baily

quickly reads it and stands up.

"Fine!" she says and smiles back at Andrea. "I am going to

go see how the lab is doing with the phone. I will see you in a little

bit," Baily says to her and leaves.

Andrea looks down at some more pictures as the hour drags

on. She must have gone through hundreds of photos and she didn't recognize anyone at all. She rubs her eyes and looks up and out of

the office. She spots Luke talking to Baily. She has her hand on his

arm and she is smiling and nodding as he spoke to her. Andrea's

stomach turns at the sight. She believes their body language shows

that they are close. Her stomach does another flip at the possibility

of Luke being with Baily. She didn't think that Luke is going out

with anyone. He hasn't mentioned anyone to her, but she didn't ask

him anything about his personal life either. Andrea searched the

house when he wasn't home. She looked for pictures. She looked for

anything that would give her a sign that he has someone special in

his life. She came up with nothing, but after seeing him with Baily,

she isn't so sure. She stares at the two of them in complete agony.

Luke finally turns to look at her and she blushes at being caught

staring. She quickly puts her head down and continues to look at the photos.

Luke listens to Baily talk about the case and wonders why he just isn't in love with her. *She has a great down to earth personality, she's smart and hot. Not to mention she is great in bed...*

"Luke, are you listening to anything I am saying?" Baily looks at him puzzled.

"Yeah, sorry." He looks back at her as Captain Corrigan steps out of his office and calls out.

"Luke, Baily in my office, now!" he commands as the two of them look at each other and shrug their shoulders. They walk into the office and there is another person in there. Someone that neither of them has ever seen before. Captain Corrigan points to a couple of chairs and each of them take a seat.

"This is Brad Beckman. He works for the NSA, and he will

from now on be working with you on this case."

"What does the NSA have to do with this?" Baily takes the words out of Luke's mouth.

"He has some information for us that we all need to hear. So wait with all the questions," Captain Corrigan replies and gestures for Beckman to begin.

"The NSA has been working with Mr. Parker for a little over a year now. Mr. Parker was able to come up with a program that used codes to break into any software program, any satellite, any computer in the entire world. I spoke with him a couple of weeks ago and he told me that he was nearly finished. The next thing that we hear, is that he is in the hospital. I couldn't come forward any earlier because it is top secret. If this program falls into the wrong hands, the security of all people in the entire world would be breached. Last night, I contacted Captain Corrigan and was told that the people behind his shooting want to get the program. I have reason to believe that a spy by the name of Gregory Prochesky is behind it all." He hands Luke the file to look at.

"What makes you say that?" Luke asks the question.

"A couple of weeks ago, he arrived in Green Hill. He traveled in from Russia under one of his many aliases, Eric Powers. As soon as we got word of that from the airport security, we sent one of our agents out to follow him, but he managed to lose him. We have no idea where he is now. Prochesky is one of the most competent people in the field of espionage in the world. He used to work with us but turned on us a few years ago. We aren't sure which government he is working for now. This case, as of now, has become top priority for NSA. We need to find the people behind this, and the flash drive. This however, needs to remain top secret. We can't afford for the news of this program to leak out. A picture of Prochesky will be given to every officer, and hopefully, we will get a lead on him. The officers will all think that they are looking for the cop killer." He hands his card to each of them. "As soon as you find anything out, please call me. I will be working on tracking Prochesky. He is obviously here for an important reason. I think someone leaked out information about the program from our department, and I will be working on an internal investigation, as well." He packs the file back in his briefcase and heads out of the office.

"Wow," Baily says, "this just gets better and better. I will be in my office if anyone needs me." She stands up to leave and Captain Corrigan responds,

"Make sure that everything that was said in this office remains here. Luke, take this picture to Miss Parker and ask her if she has ever seen him." Luke takes the picture and goes to the room where Andrea is reviewing files.

She doesn't have to look up to know that it's Luke. She feels his presence. All of her body's senses come alive when he is near her. Not to mention, she can smell the cologne that he wears.

"How's it going?"

"Just, plain, great!" Andrea answers sarcastically, without looking up at him.

"Who pissed you off?" He asks, even though he knows exactly what is bothering her. He saw the look in her eyes when he caught her looking at him with Baily. That thought made him smile. Maybe she does have some feelings for him after all. Andrea still doesn't reply. He sits on a chair right next to her, with his thigh touching hers. Her heart starts to beat faster as she feels tingles throughout her whole body.

"Andie, I asked you a question," he whispers into her ear. She is way beyond aroused. She turns her head and their eyes lock. She wants him, and the look in his eyes showed her that he wants her, too.

"No one," she quietly says. Luke backs off a little and puts the file that he was holding in front of her.

"I need you to take a look at one more photo, and then we can leave." He flips the file open and she grabs the picture. The door to the office opens again.

"Here's your phone, Miss Parker," Officer Baily says as she puts it on the table. She looks at Luke and says, "A word, Luke," she makes a gesture with her head, and Luke follows her out.

Andrea watches them through the glass. Baily tells him

something. He nods, and then he says something, and Baily smiles.

She glances at Andrea, than tells Luke something else. Luke

leans in and whispers something in Baily's ear. Baily smiles, and

nods. Andrea hates the fact that she doesn't know how to lip read.

She would have loved to hear the conversation that the two of

them just had. She looks down at the picture that Luke told her to

look at and stares at it in awe. It was a photo of Eric Powers. Andrea

met him a few months ago at the hospital in Seattle. He ran into her

and then asked her out for coffee. They went out on a few dates, but

she decided to end it there. She did like him and they had a lot in

common, but Andrea wanted a spark and she didn't have one with

him. She laid down the picture and looked up right into Luke's eyes.

"I didn't hear you come in."

"You were deep in thought. When I came in you were staring at the photo. You recognize him?" She looks up at Luke and then glances at Baily who was now standing right next to him.

"Yes, I do. His name is Eric Powers. He lives in Seattle. I met him a few months ago at the hospital. What does he have to do with any of this?" she asked puzzled.

"Did you ever talk about Matt?" Baily starts the questioning.

"Maybe, one night. We went out to dinner and talked about our families. He did ask me what Matthew does for a living. I told him that he works with computers. But that was it. I really didn't know what he did with them. After that date, we never discussed Matt again."

"How long were you dating him?" Luke jumps in, and Baily

elbows him in his side. Andrea doesn't notice how inappropriate the question is and answers.

"We dated for a couple of months, but we stopped seeing each other about a month ago. I still don't see what he has to do with anything?"

"He is just one of the people that we are looking at," Baily responds, "I am going to make a call, and I will talk to you later." She purposefully winks at Luke and leaves the office. Luke smiles and turns back to Andrea.

Chapter 6

"You ready to go?" Luke asks her as she stands up and walks right by him. She nods and quickly goes ahead of him a few steps. Luke follows her out with a big grin on his face. He feels like he's a teenager all over again. They get into his car and he said, "Let's stop somewhere and get a bite to eat before we head home. I know a great little place not too far from my house."

Andrea doesn't reply. She just nods and continues to look out of the window.

Green Hill has changed a lot since she has lived here. There were a lot more boutiques and buildings in the center of the town. The beautiful, stoned building that used to be the Court House was now the police station. A new building, which was built next to the police station, was now the Court House. They passed by a Giant

Eagle, and she turns to him.

"They even have Giant Eagle now?" she asks surprised.

"They put one here about a year ago. Green Hill is not the same town that it once was. Your brother had a lot to do with that. A lot of business men came here and opened all these new places up. So many more people have moved here. I guess that Denver has become overly populated. More and more people are moving here each year. Even during the summer months, the ski resorts are packed. " He parks in a parking lot, and leads her into Rosetta's.

It is a little restaurant filled with booths and tables. It has a bar at the far end of the restaurant, with a little TV hanging on the wall. It is a very cute and cozy place. A hostess leads them to a booth and they sit across from each other.

"I have never been in here," she says as she grabs a menu to look at. "You come here often?"

"Not as often as I would like. See anything that you would like to try?"

Andrea looks up from the menu, "what are you going to get? Everything looks good to me." She smiles at the waitress that comes over to take their orders. He asks for a hamburger with fries and a coke, and Andrea orders a tri-color pasta dish and a glass of red wine. After a couple of minutes of an awkward silence, Luke once again speaks up.

"What has gotten you so upset?"

"Nothing," Andrea replied and faked a smile. She doesn't want Luke to know what is really bothering her.

"Since you won't tell me what it is that's bothering you, why don't you tell me what I have missed out on since I have last seen you." Luke says to her non-confrontationally. Andrea tells him how she became a doctor. She tells him about Seattle, and all about Bella. As he listens to her talk about Bella, he realizes how much he has missed her voice, her smile, and her laugh. While Andrea continues to talk, Luke eats his dinner and carefully listens to her every word. He wants to know everything there is to know about her. He wants to know if and how much she has changed over the last eight years.

When she asks him questions about his life, he doesn't go into great detail. He doesn't want her to know his thoughts and feelings, he doesn't want to give himself fully to her. He has been there before and he still isn't ready to get his heart broken again. Neither of them mention the night that caused them both to have such empty, lonely lives. As Andrea finished up her glass of wine, Luke got up and paid the tab. They drove home in a comfortable silence.

Andrea used the bathroom first and headed to bed. All she could think about was Luke. She thought about that kiss and how much she wants him. She even thought about going into his room and seducing him, but she laughed that thought right out of her mind. She is in granny panties and a t-shirt; there was no way that outfit said "sexy". But God, did she want him. All he has to do is look at her and she melts. She wishes more than anything that he feels the same way. The last time she has had sex was eight years ago with Luke. She had opportunities, but no man she went out with seemed to trigger her there. She heard Luke leave his room. He paused by her room for a couple of seconds, then she heard his footsteps head downstairs. She looked at the clock, it was 2:30 a.m. After a few minutes of tossing and turning, she decided to join him downstairs.

She found him sitting in the kitchen with a cup of coffee in front of him. He was wearing a pair of grey, loose, sweat pants and a plain white t-shirt. Without a word she made her way to the coffee pot and poured herself a cup.

"Andie," he whispered standing right behind her and she jumped causing her to spill some of the coffee on the counter. She put the cup down and turned around. Her eyes started to darken and her heart started to beat so fast and so strong, that she thought it was going to explode. "Andie," he sighs and shakes his head. "You can't just walk around me dressed like this." He said to her in that soft, slow, sexy voice of his. "Don't you know how beautiful and sexy you are?" He put his hand on her cheek and caressed her lips with his thumb. "Don't you know how bad I want you?" He slowly kisses her cheek, then the corner of her mouth, then the other side of her mouth. He held her chin up so that she's looking directly into his eyes. "I want you, Andie."

She swallows, puts her arms around his neck and kisses him. Their tongues explore each others' mouths. He pulls her knee up and his hand slides up her leg to her underwear. He grabs her ass and pins her to him so that she could feel his erection against her sex. He removes her shirt and put his mouth back on hers. With his hand on her breast, he flicks her nipple with his thumb, then pulls on it. She thought she was going to explode right then and there. He nibbles her ear lobe.

"God, you're beautiful," he whispered in her ear. With his mouth back on hers, he lifts her into his arms and takes her up to his bedroom. He gently lays her on the bed and gets on top of her. "Andie, are you sure you want to do this?"

"Yes, Luke, I want this more than anything." She replies, and his mouth claims hers once more. He kisses her neck, then he slowly kisses and licks his way down. Down to her all ready perked up breasts. "Ahhh," she moans and arches her back. He sucks on her breast while his fingers play with her clitoris. He inserts one finger, then two inside of her while his thumb flicks her soft spot. He continues to do this and she starts to build. Her insides started to quiver and tighten and then she explodes. He quickly puts on a condom, spreads her legs wide and goes in. He starts to slowly penetrate. She feels him go in deeper and deeper. She lifts her hips and clenches her muscles. He speeds up the pace and she matches him thrust for thrust. She starts to build again. A couple of more thrusts and she burst once again. He feels her come, and with one more plunge, he lets go. He just had the most mind blowing orgasm of his life. He closes his eyes and holds her a bit longer. After their breathing returns to normal, he withdraws from her, and lies down beside her. He turns her around and wraps his arm around her. He holds her tight, and falls asleep. She hasn't felt like this in years. She is totally sedated and calm. She is in heaven. She wants to be with him forever.

The following morning she woke up in his arms. Without wanting to disturb him, she gently lifts his arms from around her chest, carefully slips out of bed, dresses, and heads downstairs. She put on a pot of coffee and started to make breakfast. She's making Luke's favorite today; bacon and French toast. At least that used to be his favorite, she thought. She wonders exactly if and how much he has changed over the last few years. Just as she finished making breakfast, he casually strolls into the kitchen. He is wearing a black pair of jeans, and a dark blue dress shirt that was rolled up to his

elbows.

"Good morning." He says with a big grin on his face. She

blushes and he grabs her. With his arms wrapped around her, he

gently kisses her, then sucks and nibbles her lower lip teasing her.

She places her hands on the back of his head and plays with his hair.

"Good morning." She says as her body gets ready again.

"Hmmm…." Luke grunts and reluctantly releases her and

pulls away. She sticks her bottom lip out and pouts. "Don't pout,

Andie. You know if we go to bed now we'll never leave

the bedroom. We need to find that flash drive. We need to catch

these guys before someone else gets hurt." He makes his way to the

counter and takes a seat. Andrea places the food on their plates and

puts one in front of him, and one in front of herself. They start to eat and she asks,

"Do you have any suspects yet?"

"They are re-interviewing all his contacts as we speak. They are going to let me know if they come up with any leads. I figure our best bet of catching them, is finding the flash drive. When you guys were younger, did your brother have a hiding spot?" Andrea thought about it for a few minutes.

"Matt's favorite place used to be the tree house in our backyard. My dad made it when we were little. That tree house was his sanctuary by the time he was a teenager. He wouldn't let anyone in there, including me. Which reminds me, did the police check the cabin? Maybe he hid it there."

"Yeah, we did a thorough check of the cabin, too. Nothing was found there, either. Well, I guess we can start with the tree house. It's the only place no one thought to look. So let's finish up our breakfast, and we will head out to the tree house."

She cleared the table and ran up to shower and change. She put on a pair of light blue jeans, and a black v-neck sweater that showed a little bit of cleavage. She quickly tied up her hair, put on her white tennis shoes and met up with Luke who was waiting for her in the car.

Chapter 7

"Do you know if Julia and Matt were having any marital problems?" Luke asks her as they drive out to the house.

"No, not that I know of. I know that they have been spending a lot of time and money at some fertility clinic. They have been trying to have a baby the last three years. Julia has had two miscarriages already. Why do you ask?"

"Just wondering," Luke replies as he parks the car in the driveway. They walk around into the house because Andrea remembered seeing a key ring marked "tree house" hanging in a kitchen closet. They grabbed the key ring wondering why so many keys were on it and head straight to the backyard. The tree house is built in a huge maple tree. The tree house looked the same as it did before, but there was an additional tree house built in a tree set back further back on the property. The two tree houses were connected by a wooden walkway. From the house, you wouldn't be able to see the expansion at all. The leaves on the trees covered everything. Matthew hid the place well; at least in the summer, but in the fall and winter months it would be another story.

"Wow, Andie, this is awesome!"

"That's exactly what I was thinking. The other tree house looks huge!" Andrea heads up the ladder and starts to try keys in the lock. The second one opened the door that lead into the first house and Luke follows her in. As Andrea steps in and looks around she smiles. "Matt hasn't changed a thing in here. It looks exactly the same as it did when I was young." She smiles at the thought that Matt didn't want to change the tree house, after all, it was their dad who had made it. She walked to the door that led to the walkway to the other house. "Are you coming?" she asks him as she turns

around to look at him. Luke was walking around and checking

everything out.

"Yeah, you go ahead. I will catch up with you. I just want to

search through everything in here first."

"All right, suit yourself. I want to check out the other house. I

have never seen anything like this!" She heads out and Luke

continues to look around. There was nothing in here that he didn't

expect to see. There were a couple of posters on the wall, a little

wooden barrel in the middle, and one big wooden chest in the corner.

He opened up the chest and looked through it. No flash drive, just a

bunch of old magazines, and a BB gun. The barrel that was in the

middle of the room was empty. *Where did he put that flash drive?*

Frustrated that he came up empty, he decided to meet up with

Andrea in the other tree house.

He opened the door and halts in awe. This is the coolest place he had ever seen. The house is actually an office. It has a big, dark wooden desk, with a laptop in the middle. There is a smaller desk with a printer, fax machine, and other computer towers spread out all over it in a corner. There is a huge window overlooking the mountains. He turned his head to the left and sees another door that Andrea had walked out of.

"Wow!" She exclaims. "What an office! This place is amazing! It even has a bathroom. I wonder how much time Matthew actually spends in here?" Luke walks in and closes the door.

"I wish that my office would look like this!" He exclaims as he walks over to the desk. He turns on the computer at and waits.

"Damn it. I can't get on it without a password. It looks

like this baby is going to the police station with me." He continues to

search through the desk, and comes up empty. He walks over to the

other desk and goes through each drawer, but no flash drive. He

pulls out his phone and places a call.

"Hey Cap, we just found a hidden office up in a tree house in

the back of the Parker residence. I am going to need a couple of

officers to help me bring all of this computer equipment down."

"Okay, I will send someone ASAP. You call up Beckman

and tell him what you have found. Tell him that everything will be at

the station. If he wants to send anyone out to examine it, he can."

Cap hangs up.

Luke looks over at Andrea who was staring out of the

window admiring the view.

"I am going to step outside for a minute, I need to make

another phone call." He quickly goes out on the ramp and closes the door behind him. He doesn't want Andrea to hear his conversation with Beckman. As he hangs up the phone, he hears a loud thump and a scream. He runs back in and sees Andrea lying on the floor. Luke kneels beside her.

"What happened?"

"I stumbled and I twisted my ankle. It's throbbing!" She rubs her ankle and looks at it.

"Can you make it up? You want to go to the hospital?" She gives him a dirty look and rolls her eyes.

"I am a doctor, remember? I do know how to take care of it!" She snaps at him, than regrets her snapping. She doesn't want to upset him. "Sorry, I'll be fine. I will just put some ice on it when we get home. Do you have an ice pack in the freezer?"

"Yes, I do, even a couple of them. But what happened?" He

asks her again and her face turns bright red out of embarrassment.

"I don't know. I tripped on that little stump over there in the

corner." She points to a piece of wood sticking out of the wooden

floor by the small desk. He helps her stand up, and he walks over to

the little stump. He presses on it and a piece of wood flooring slides

open. They both take a minute to process what they see. Beneath it

is a compartment with a box in it.

"Your brother is one smart man. We just got lucky. If you

didn't stumble upon this, no one would have found this

compartment." He takes the box out. It is a little steel safe that opens

by a security code. "We need to try to open it. Do you have any idea

as to what he would use as the password?"

"I can try," she answers and takes the box from him. She puts in Matthew's birthday, then his social security number, then she tried

Julia's, as well as her own, and nothing so far worked. Fifteen

minutes passed by and the tree house is flooded with men in

uniform.

"I will take that." Officer Baily says to her as she extends her

hands toward it. "This is going to the station for processing. We are

going to try to open it up there."

Andrea hands it over to her, stands up and puts all of her

weight on her left foot. *I wish I could have opened up that safe. I*

would love to know what that safe holds. The police took all of

the electronic equipment out and the last of the officers just exited

the tree house. Luke is standing at the doorway.

"Come on. We can go." He motions to her as she hobbles

over to him. He lets her lead the way. Slowly, but surely, they finally make it to the other tree. They enter the other house and go out of the door. Andrea sighs at the sight of the ladder. She turns back and looks at him.

"How about you go first?"

"All right," and he starts his way down the ladder.

She follows him down, taking her time. Her foot is throbbing. She can't wait to get home, take an Advil and put some ice on it. Half way down the ladder, she loses her grip and tumbles backward right into his arms.

"Thank you," she said to him as he steadied her on the ground.

"You're welcome. Are you sure you don't want to stop at the hospital?" he asked her again.

"No, I will be okay. I just twisted my ankle, I didn't break it."

"Geez, Andie, I bet you wouldn't go to the hospital even if your leg was broken." He shakes his head at her. She grabs his arm and he helps her get to the car.

They drive out onto the street and make a right at the intersection. After a few streets, Luke notices a black SUV a couple of cars behind them. The windows are tinted and he can't see the driver. He moved into the other lane, and the SUV followed suit.

"I think we're being followed."

"Are you sure?" she asked him as she turned to look through the back window.

"Nope, but we will find out in a minute." He made a left turn at the next light. The SUV followed. Luke sped up a little and so did the car. He got on his cell and phones Cap.

"We are being followed."

118

"Give me the license plate number," Cap answers back.

"It's RT 569 AP Colorado plate." Luke hangs up. "Don't worry about anything," he says to Andrea who was looking straight ahead and tugging on her earlobe with her right hand. "I'm going to drive to the police station, and maybe he will follow us all of the way there." He sped up on the ramp and got onto the freeway. Luke drove the speed limit so that Andrea doesn't freak out even more. All of a sudden, the SUV rams right into them, forcing the car to jerk.

"What the hell!" Luke angrily yells out as he looks in the rearview mirror. He still couldn't make out the driver. He speeds up a little and the SUV moves into the right lane. The SUV rams into the car on Andrea's side and she screams.

Scoot down, Andie, and stay down!" Luke orders. He floors

the car and goes way ahead of the SUV. She sits back and grips the

door handle with her right hand, and braces her left on the

dashboard. She closes her eyes and prays. Andie hates speeding cars,

and she hates them even more after the car accident that claimed her

parents' lives. The only reason that she bought the house in Seattle

was because it is within walking distance to the hospital, and to the

shopping center. Andrea drove only where she had to because of

weather conditions, or the time of day. She is lucky that nothing is

far from where she lives. His phone rings and he picks it up.

"Yeah."

"The car belongs to someone named Christian Barnes. He

reported it stolen about two and a half weeks ago. I sent a squad car

to get him. I want you to come to the station."

"We are almost there." He hangs up, and grips the steering

wheel.

"Hang on Andie, we are going to get off at the next exit."

The driver of the SUV is a lot smarter than Luke thought. He knows that Luke is headed to the police station so he slows down and is now far behind them. Luke gets off the freeway, but this time, the SUV fails to follow. He slows down to the speed limit.

"He didn't follow us out, Andie, we are almost at the station." Shaking, she forces herself to look back.

"It's okay," he grabs her hand and kisses her knuckles in an attempt to calm her down.

"I will tell you what, when we leave the station, we will stop at the hospital and then we'll head home. We'll order some pizza, and watch a movie like the good old days. I have cable and I will even let you pick out the movie." He smiles at her and she nods okay.

At the station, Luke leaves Andrea in his office and he goes

to talk with Captain Corrigan. He enters Cap's office.

"Did anyone pick up the SUV?" Luke asks.

"No," Cap disappointedly answers. "Ryan was just a few car

lengths behind you. He saw you take the exit and he followed the

SUV. He said that the vehicle exited at the next exit, but that he lost

him somewhere downtown."

"That's just great!" Luke says sarcastically to Cap.

"I put out an APB on the vehicle. We will be bringing

Christian Barnes in for questioning."

"Is anyone going through the things we took out of the tree

house yet? How about the safe?"

"They are going through everything right now. Beckman

should be here soon. He has a computer expert that works for the

NSA coming in, too. As soon as they open it, I will let you know."

Meanwhile, Andrea is sitting at Luke's desk. To distract herself, and out of curiosity, she starts to open up the drawers and look through his things. His office says dull. There are no pictures anywhere, and the desk top is neat and cleared off. He has a laptop on it, but it is shut off. There is a file cabinet and one more chair. *Luke doesn't bring his personal life into the office, and he doesn't bring his work home*, she thought. After a few minutes of just sitting there, Officer Baily stops in and takes a seat.

"Did you get a look at the driver?" she asks Andrea.

"No, the windows were tinted, I couldn't see anything, and to tell you the truth, I was too scared to even look."

"Luke is the best detective we have here, so you are in good hands. I notice that something is going on with you two. I suggest that you stay away from him," Baily says. Andrea,

shocked, looks at her.

"I really don't know what you are talking about. My personal

life is really not of your concern."

"No, you are right. It's not my business, but don't say I didn't

warn you." Baily stands up as Luke walks into his office. "Hi Luke,

is everything ready?"

"The report is all done. I assume that you will do the

questioning when they bring in Barnes, and the driver. So give me a

call when it's all over. I am going to head out to the hospital

now, and then I should be home the rest of the day."

"No problem, I will give you a call as soon as I can. I'm

glad you are okay. You need to be a little more careful. You know

how much I worry about you!" Baily says to Luke as she taps

his chest. "I will talk and see you later." She walked away.

Andrea just sat there and had observed the two of them. *Their body language said a lot, and they were both flirting with each other. They seem like they are more than just two people that work together. They seem pretty close. There is something going on with the two of them! Was Baily warning her because she has something going on with Luke or was she warning her for another reason?*

"Thanks, Baily!" He calls out to her. She turns around and smiles at him.

He sticks his hand out to Andrea and instead of taking it, she gets up and limps out of the station with Luke right behind her. She didn't say a word when they got into the car.

"Off to the hospital!" He exclaims and looks at her as he starts the car. She doesn't look at him.

"What's the matter, Andie?"

"What's with you and Baily?" she asks.

"Why do you think that there is something going on with us?"

"She told me to stay away from you, and I don't know what I saw going on between the two of you. I was right there you know!" she exclaims.

He looks at her and shakes his head.

"Andie, Andie, Andie! There is nothing going on between the two of us. We are just friends. We actually dated a few months ago. But I ended it. I didn't think it was such a good idea."

"So you don't like her?"

"No, not in that way." He grabs her hand.

"I am only in to you, sweetheart."

Luke parks the car in the hospital parking lot and they get out of it.

He watches Andrea limp to the elevator. "I see your ankle still

hurts." He presses the fourth floor button and the elevator door

closes.

"Yes, it's swollen now. I need to put ice on it." They get off

on their floor and walk over to Matt's room. Luke waited outside

while she went in to visit. Matt looked the same as he did yesterday.

Andrea checked his chart and then took a seat right next to him.

"Come on Matty, snap out of it, please!" She grabs his hand.

"I need you. Please don't leave me."

The door opens and Dr. Newman walks into the room.

"How are you doing, Dr. Parker?"

"I'm okay. I am just running out of patience. It has been five

days, and he hasn't budged," she replies. "I just wish that he would wake up."

"I know you do, and he will, I am sure. He just isn't ready to come back into our world. It is taking him a little bit longer than usual. As long as his vitals stay like this, I wouldn't worry so much."

"I know, I just can't help it, he is my brother." She smiles at Dr. Newman.

"We are only human! Sometimes we just can't help how we feel. If you need anything or have any questions at all, I will be on the floor the rest of the night." Dr. Newman replies, and leaves the room. After a few more minutes, Andrea says her good bye to Matt and steps into the hallway to join Luke.

"You ready to go?" Luke asked, surprised that she wasn't there too long.

"Yes, I really need to ice my ankle."

Luke makes it home in record time. Once they step into the house, Andrea enters the kitchen and grabs an ice pack out of the freezer. She takes it to the living room and puts it on her ankle. Luke meanwhile, ordered pizza and got their drinks ready. Twenty minutes later, the pizza arrived. Luke pays for it and sets the boxes on the kitchen counter. He takes out a couple of spinach and cheese pieces for Andrea, and two pepperoni slices for himself which he places on a plate.

Luke hands her the plate filled with pizza and sits right next to her on the couch.

"Did you find a movie yet?"

"No, not yet," Andrea continues to look at the guide. "I don't see anything interesting on the list."

"Good," he smile, "I really didn't feel like watching one. I want to take a shower, and I want to go to bed." He takes a bite out of his pizza and wonders if she got the hint. Andrea, however, puts the show 'Criminal Minds' on and begins to watch it.

"Do you ever watch this show?" She asks him as she digs into the pizza.

"Nope. To tell you the truth, I never have the time. I usually just come home to sleep and shower."

"What do you do when you are on vacation?"

"I usually go camping in the mountains. I have this great spot that I go to every time," he replies, "What do you do when you have time off?"

"I just spend it at home. I spend a lot of time with Bella. You know, the neighbor that I have told you about." She places her empty plate on the table.

"You want me to bring you some more?"

"No thanks, the pizza was really good, but I have had enough."

Luke gets up and takes the plates to the kitchen. He puts the rest of the pizza in the fridge, and then goes back to his spot on the couch. He sticks his hand behind her and moves her closer. Andrea gets comfortable and places her head on his shoulder. After a couple of minutes, Luke starts to feel a little antsy. He smells her hair and closes his eyes. He sure loves the way her hair smells, like fresh apples. He wants this moment to last forever. She belongs with him and in his arms, he thought. For a moment, his mind travels to the past. He never understood why she said 'no' that night. Luke was so angry with himself and at her, that he didn't even ask her why. He simply figured that she didn't love him. On the way home that night from the hotel, Andrea tried to explain it to him. Every time she opened her mouth to say something, he cut her off. Last night, when they made love, he saw the love in her eyes. He saw that she wanted him. *So why did Andie say no?* He wonders. Does he really want to know? Just thinking about that night hurts him. Maybe, one day he will ask her, but not any time soon. It is still a sore subject to Luke. She's back into his life, and he's glad. He hopes to do whatever it takes to keep her this time. He just needs to make sure that she feels the same way about him. Every now and then when he looks at her, he remembers that horrid night. Every time he has thought about that night, all he did was upset himself. When he thought about that night, he remembers how he became angry at her and at himself. He was mad that she said no, and he is still mad at her for hurting him. Andrea nudges him, and he opens his eyes.

"You aren't sleeping, are you?"

"No, I was just thinking."

"What were you thinking about?" her curiosity takes over.

"Nothing in particular." He doesn't want to talk about that night, just yet. Right now, he just wants to enjoy the time he has with her. He lifts her up on his lap placing his hand on her leg and starts to slowly rub her thigh. His hand travels from the knee all of the way up to her hip and back again. She puts her head under his chin and presses her cheek into his neck. Luke starts to slowly rub the back of her thigh. As he reaches for her behind, Andie moves a little, and Luke's manhood starts to grow.

"Luke?"

"Yes, Andie" he says in that voice that sets her body on fire.

"I take it you don't really want to watch the show?" She looks at him and he presses his lips to hers. Slowly he teases her with his lips. He licks, then nips her lower lip.

"Ahhh…" she groans. As her mouth widens his tongue goes in and he kisses her deeper and more forcefully. She holds him tighter not wanting to let go. She wants him bad. She starts to untuck his shirt from his pants, but he stops her.

"Not here, lets' go upstairs." She gets up and moves out of his way limping. He starts to laugh.

"What's so funny?" she asks him as she turns back to look at him.

"You," he says as he lifts her in his arms. He carries her up the stairs. He pushes the door open with his foot and gently sits her on the bed. He takes off her shirt, unhooks her bra, and lays her on the bed as he gets on top of her. He kisses her earlobe and then nips it. He works his way down her neck and down to her breast. He pulls and tugs on her nipple with his fingers and then puts his mouth on it. He licks and flicks her nipple with his tongue, then sucks and tugs on it with his teeth. After a couple of minutes he moves to her other breast. Andrea is in bliss. Her body starts to move; her hips start to sway and his erection rubs her through his jeans. He slowly and carefully takes her sweats off along with her underwear. He lifts her behind and starts to lick the most sensitive spot on her whole body. She clutches the sheets with her hands and explodes. She opens her eyes and smiles at him.

"I think it's my turn now," she says with a hoarse voice. She wants to lick and taste every inch of him. He takes off his clothes and lies down on the bed as she sits up. She clutches his manhood. She feels his hard erection and licks the top and then takes him in.

She uses her hands and her lips as she sucks and licks. Just as he was reaching his climax, he pulls her up and places her on top of him. She starts to move and with each move he goes in deeper. With each move she feels him reaching toward her heart. Surprising her, he sits up and cups her face. She opens her eyes and looks right into his.

"I love you," he softly says. "I always did and I always will." Without giving her a chance to reply, he puts his mouth on hers and she holds him tight as they both simultaneously come. Completely sated and utterly happy, she dozes off in his arms.

Chapter 8

Luke set off on his morning routine. He's been neglecting his usual run in the morning. It's been four days since he stepped into his sneakers. He likes to use his running time to think things through. He had received a late night call from Cap and Baily updating him on the team's progress on the case. Cap said that they didn't find the SUV, but the APB is still out. Baily told him that Barnes' alibi checks out, and that he did report the car stolen a couple of weeks ago. *Great*, Luke thought. The man who called Andrea the other day hasn't called back yet, either. The number that was used to call her was from a burner phone. They haven't been able to open up the safe yet, either. We have no idea if the flash drive is even in there.

Luke enters the house and sees that Andrea is in the kitchen talking on the phone. He pours himself a cup of coffee and waits for her to get off the phone.

"Thank you for calling, I will be right there," Andrea says as she hangs up the phone, and turns to Luke. "That was Dr. Newman, Matt woke up from the coma about an hour ago. She said she checked him out and he seems to be doing fine. The only problem is that he can't remember anything that happened the night of the home invasion."

"How's your ankle?"

"Better, but still sore. As soon as I get into other clothes, I would like to go see Matt."

"Okay, I will be ready to go in fifteen minutes." Luke ran up the stairs to shower and change.

In the car, on the way to the hospital, he calls Cap and tells him the news. "I will interview him when I get there, and I will give you a report when I finish. See you then," Luke hangs up.

"Andie, I am going to need to ask Matt some questions, I will need a few minutes alone with him. Maybe it would be better that I talk with him first."

"I understand, I will wait outside of the room. But please don't take too long." They park the car, get on the elevator, and head up to the room. Luke greets Officer Ryan and enters the room, while Andrea goes in search of Dr. Newman. Luke extends his hand and says,

"Mr. Parker, I am…"

"No need for the formality, Luke. I might not be able to remember what happened that night, but I do remember everything that happened eight years ago. Where's Julia? Is Andrea here, too?" Matt interrupts him.

"Andie went to find the doctor. I was hoping that I could ask you some questions first, without her being here. Julia was kidnapped that night. Someone called Andie and told her that she needed to get some flash drive. If she doesn't, he is going to kill Julia. It's been three days since that phone call. The man hasn't called her back yet. Do you remember anything about that day?"

"I remember that I worked for a few hours, and then Julia and I went to a fundraiser. We came back around 11 p.m. because Julia wasn't feeling well. That's all I remember, and here I am."

"Have you and Julia been having any problems?"

"To tell you the truth, the last few months have been tough. I thought that Julia was acting pretty strange, so I hired a private investigator to follow her around about six weeks ago. He brought me a lot of pictures of her with another man. I told her that I wanted a divorce. She said that she loved me and that she was sorry. She even said that she would go to counseling and begged me to forgive her. I told her that I would think about it. About a month ago I had my lawyer draw up the divorce papers. When I handed them to her, she actually laughed and said that there was no way in hell that she would sign them. I told her that she had two months to move out. I didn't even expect her to go to the fundraiser, but Julia loves those things. I didn't mention anything to Andrea about this at all. I would appreciate it if you don't say anything to her about it either. I would like to be the one to tell her."

"That's not a problem Matt, I have a feeling that Julia is involved in this somehow. We just can't seem to find her. The NSA thinks that a spy is behind all of this."

"Did you find the flash drive?"

"If it is in the safe that you had in the tree house, then yes. Otherwise we didn't."

"Yes, that's exactly where it is. Damn it! I have to call Brad Beckman." Matthew starts to panic.

"He should actually be on his way." Luke looks down at his watch. "Do you know the man that Julia was having an affair with?"

"His name is Jeff Hughes. He works for the mayor. Can I see Andrea now? I'm getting pretty tired."

"Yeah, sure, I will send her right in," Luke opens the door and says, "Andie, he's ready to see you." She goes in to see Matt.

"Matt!!" She screams in delight, and runs over to him. She carefully hugs him and kisses him on the cheek. "How are you feeling? I have been so worried. I don't know what I would have done if you left me, too." The tears start to flow from her eyes.

"I will be just fine," he says to her as he grabs her hand. "Dr. Newman thinks that, other than some pain, everything will be okay."

"They have checked your brain activity and everything seems normal." She smiles at him. After about a half an hour, Luke returns and tells them that he is going to run to the police station. He wants to check out Jeff Hughes. As he turned to leave, Beckman walks in.

"Don't go anywhere yet, Luke. I will head out to the station and I would like you to join me there."

"Okay, no problem," Luke replies and sits down on a chair.

"Matthew!" Beckman shakes his hand. "I am so glad that you will be all right."

"Brad, that flash drive is in the safe."

"I figured as much. We can't open it up though. They have been working on it for the last 16 hours. Patton figured out the first code, but that's as far as he got." He takes out a little notebook and a pen. "Ready."

"It's 07468, then 89251, and then there is a problem." They all anxiously stare at him. "After the second password goes through, a little image appears in the screen. It asks for a fingerprint. The box will only open up with my fingerprint."

"Great." Beckman states and grabs his phone and makes a call. "I will need that safe pronto. Bring it to the hospital. I will wait for it downstairs," then hangs up. "I guess we will all just have to sit and wait. It should be here in twenty minutes."

"You really think that a spy is after it?" Matthew asks.

"Not a 100% sure, but I believe so."

"How about Julia?"

"There are more people involved then just the spy, that's for sure. I don't know about Julia. The police are investigating everything that has to do with the case. My main concern is Prochesky. My team is trying to track him down. This flash drive can't fall into the wrong hands. If it does, every government agency, every bank, every person's identity is at risk." Beckman replies. "I will go downstairs and wait for it. I will be back as soon as I get the safe."

"Well, since we will be here a while longer, I am going to run over to the cafeteria and grab us all some coffee." Luke says and walks out of the room, leaving Andrea alone with Matt.

As soon as Luke closes the door, Andrea turns towards him.

"Why would you ask if Julia might be involved?

"It's a long story, Andrea, and I am really tired. I am going to close my eyes and relax for a few minutes."

145

Chapter 9

He sits in his car and takes a hit on the cigarette that he just lit up. *God that feels so good. Julia has been driving me crazy. Not to mention the two idiots that I hired to help me are totally hopeless.* He takes another drag. He has been sitting here in the parking lot of the hospital, since he heard about Matthew waking up. He needs and wants that flash drive. He doesn't care about the money he can make off of it, he cares about the power he will have because of it. *Every government agency will want it, and pretty soon the whole world will be eating out of my palm. But because the two retards couldn't find it, I now have to come up with plan B. It is going to be a little tougher than I had thought.* He finishes his cigarette and flings it out of the window. His cell phone rings and he answers,

"Powers."

"It's Patton. The safe is on the move to the hospital. Mr.

Parker is going to open it up there."

"I figured as much when you told me that Mr. Parker awoke.

Thanks for the call, I owe you." He hangs up.

Pat Patton, has worked for the NSA for the last forty years.

Only recently, he became sick of it all. He was sick of doing the

ground work and not getting the glory that he so richly deserves.

Now that he is nearing his retirement, he wants to have more money,

as well, in the bank. He wants to travel and see the world. He was a

"desk jockey," who never got out of the office, and to his

satisfaction, he was never given credit for doing his job. Finally, he

was going to strike it rich. Calling Prochesky was the best thing that

he has ever done. The two of them, together, were going to make

millions.

Two men in dark suits get out of a car with government

plates, and head to the hospital entrance. Beckman greets them at the

door.

"Thanks for bringing it by," he says as he takes it. "You two

coming up?"

"No. We got a hit on Prochesky that we are going to check

up on. He was spotted at a hotel by the airport," one of the men

responds.

"Let me know if you get him," Beckman calls out to them as

the elevator doors close. He greets the officer by the door of the

room and knocks before he enters. Luke and Andrea were waiting

patiently, as Matthew slept. He wakes up Matt and hands the safe

over to him. "Come on, open it."

Matt puts in the first code, then the second one, and the

finger print screen comes on. He puts the safe on his lap and puts his thumb on the screen. They all watch as the top slides over and opens. He sticks his right hand inside and one by one, pulls out the content; a little black notebook, a couple of computer discs, and finally, the flash drive.

"Here it is." He hands it to Beckman. "Don't lose it. I don't have another copy." He winks at him.

Beckman knew that Matt would only make one copy of the configurations. Beckman knows that Matthew has it all memorized and is currently working on variables that would disable the systems in case these codes got into the wrong hands. But he does have to be careful. It will take as fast as a minute to get into a computer system and transfer all of the data out of it. His phone rings and he answers it.

"Beckman here…yeah… I will meet you at the station." He hangs up. "I need to go to the station. Can you give me a ride, Luke?"

"Yes, I need to go there, too." He looks over at Andrea. "Are you coming, too?"

"No. I want to stay here a while longer. I will call you when I am ready to leave. Okay?" Luke nods, and the two of them leave.

At the station, Luke and Beckman go separate ways. Luke meets up with Cap. As he takes a seat in Cap's office, he asks,

"Did you question Jeff Hughes, yet?"

"Yes, Baily did. He's not our guy. He has an air tight alibi. The only thing he confessed was the affair that he was having with Julia. He has no idea about any program or flash drive. He said that he and Julia never discussed Matt or his work. He left about 15 minutes ago."

"This is all starting to drive me crazy! I just can't figure it out. This whole time I thought that Julia was somehow behind it all. Now I think it's all Prochesky. It makes sense that it would be a spy. All the tracks were covered. But Andrea heard two men that night that she was at the hotel. So if it is Prochesky, he isn't working alone. What sucks is that all the leads that we have are pieces of a puzzle we can't seem to put together!" Luke stands up.

"I know what you mean. We'll figure it out. I just hope that no one else gets hurt."

"I am going to go check in with Beckman. He said that they got a hit on Prochesky, I want to go see what came up." He leaves Cap's office and joins Beckman in another office down the hall.

"Any news?"

"I got a call. Prochesky was using the hotel room for sure, but no one was in it when my team arrived. They should be coming in soon with the evidence they found in the room. I have someone who will stay there and be on the lookout. I figure if he left anything of importance in the room, he will have to go back to retrieve it. But 50 to 1, what evidence that we have secured from that room is of no consequence to Prochesky or us. He may have left it behind to divert our attention. He's probably moved on to a different hotel, and won't be back."

"Okay, I will head out then. Let me know if anything goes down."

"Will do."

Luke looks at his watch, and it is already 6:00p.m. Andrea still hasn't called so he figures he will go home, take a shower, and wait for her to call him there.

He pulls in his driveway, and notices that there is a light on upstairs. He thought he turned off all the lights before they left this morning. He exits the car, and carefully shuts the door. He quietly walks to the front door and sees that it is secure. He continues to the back of the house where he finds the door jamb splintered. He takes his gun out and slowly enters the house. The furniture downstairs was thrown everywhere and he hears noises coming from his bedroom upstairs. He quietly makes his way up the stairs. The door to the room is cracked open, and he stands in place to listen. There is only one man in there. He decides to make his move, storming into the room.

"Freeze! This is the police." The man halts and puts his hands up.

"Slowly turn around. Who are you? What are you doing here?"

"My name is Jeff Hughes. I know that I told your people that I know nothing about the flash drive. I lied. I am looking for it." Hughes replies and he looks as if he is going to shit in his pants.

"Why exactly are you looking for it?" Luke places a phone call and waits for his unit to respond.

"I asked you, why were you looking for the flash drive, Jeff? I want you to start talking now, and it better be the truth." Jeff Hughes works for the Mayor. Luke continues to believe that Jeff Hughes is still a suspect. Hughes is 6 feet and 2 inches tall, and skinny. He has dark hair and dark brown eyes. He tells Luke he met Julia at a coffee shop and that he instantly fell in love with her. They were going to run away with each other. They had it all planned out.

Two months ago Julia broke up with him and told him that she couldn't leave Matt.

"I was pretty upset when she ended it," he tells Luke. "I must have called her a million times the first few days after that. But the last time I called her, someone else answered her phone. He told me he was going to kill me, and I believed it. So I stopped calling, and I haven't talked to Julia since. This morning I received a call. He told me that if I wanted to save Julia's life, I need to find the flash drive. The caller said that he would keep in touch. I figured, if I found it, I could save Julia."

The police walk in and cuff him.

"Take him downtown and arrest him for breaking and entering," Luke says to his buddy Hal. "Make sure that you get his phone records. I'm off to the hospital now, and will pick up Andrea.

Call me if you need me. I will be in the office tomorrow morning, so I will make a police report then."

"I just want Julia back that's all. I'm sorry, please don't arrest me. I work for the mayor for Christ's sake! Do you know how bad this is? I'm gonna lose my job!" Jeff rambles on as the police take him away. Luke decides to make a couple of phone calls before he heads out of the house. He first called Cap and told him what happened, and then he phoned Beckman.

"I think we need to take another look at Jeff Hughes," Luke says to Beckman. "He has revealed his knowledge of the flash drive."

"It looks like he is going to stay on our list of suspects. I just hope that word about this program doesn't leak out to too many people. The President doesn't want anyone to know that we have the power to control just about everything. We need to be

really careful when we question him. Thanks for the call, and keep

me posted." Beckman hangs up.

Chapter 10

Matt tells Andrea about his failed marriage; Julia's affair, and the divorce papers waiting for her signature. Something was missing between him and Julia. Matthew has locked away his love for Julia by devoting so much time to his "computer world".

With tears in her eyes she says,

"How come you didn't tell me about Julia before?"

"I didn't feel like being lectured by you. Not to mention that it is totally humiliating. I was planning to tell you when all of the paperwork was signed and she had moved out. Oh, when it was all over, then I could appreciate your sympathy. I figured you would feel sorry for me, rather than possibly trying to keep us together. We just lost something over the years. I blame myself for the affair. I never gave her the attention that she wanted and needed."

"Oh, Matty, I am so happy that you have made it. I love you so much. I just want you to be happy. You deserve to be happy," Andrea smiles at him.

Matt smiles back at her and says,

"It's unbelievable, Andrea! I never thought that you and Luke would ever get back together again. It's amazing how life works sometimes, isn't it?"

"It sure is. How are you feeling? Are you tired? Do you want to sleep? It's 8:30, Luke is probably still at work."

"I'm okay, the pain meds are working. I'm just tired, that's all. I can't wait to get out of here."

"Well, if everything stays like this, you should be out of here in 48 hrs. If you don't mind, I would like to stay a little bit longer." She grabs his hand as Matthew falls back asleep.

159

———— * ———— * ————

As he glances in the rearview mirror, Luke spots a black

SUV. *This has got to be the same SUV*. He makes a right at the

corner and notices that the SUV does the same. *I am so going*

to get you this time. He makes a left turn at the next light, and the

SUV follows. He continues straight a couple of blocks and makes a

left at an intersection. The car is still behind him. He sees a grocery

store on his left and turns into the parking lot. He parks his car as

close as he can to the entrance, and waits to see if the SUV does the

same. The SUV goes into a parking space a few cars down. Luke

exits his vehicle and goes into the store. He hides by the door behind

a display and peers out to see if the guy follows him in. Five minutes passed, and no one got out of the SUV. He decides to use a car that just pulled up to the door, for cover. From there, he quickly makes his way toward the parked SUV. It's a good thing that it has gotten dark outside. He stays low, draws his gun, and as quickly as he can, he opens up the driver's door. He hits the man on the head with the butt of his gun, knocking him out. He pushes him into the passenger seat, climbs into the car, and shuts the door. He handcuffs the perp to the door, and goes through his pockets and takes out his wallet. Tom Reilly, 5feet and 11inches, and 26 yrs. old. He has short, dark hair which is so dark that it is almost black. Reilly moans and comes to. Luke elbows him in the ribs.

"Oww, man, would you stop hitting me," he pleads with Luke.

"I'll stop hitting you, when you start talking. You are lucky I don't do more damage to you. Why are you following me?"

"I wasn't following you, I swear. I was sitting here minding

my own business. I don't have to tell you shit. Am I under arrest? I

won't talk to you without my lawyer present." Reilly mouths off.

"Great," Luke says and punches him in his side one more

time. He calls Cap and they wait for back up. Meanwhile, Luke tries

to ask him some more questions, but he stays mum. Cap and two

more squad cars come quickly. Cap walks over to the passenger side

and gets Reilly out of the car.

"Tom Reilly, you are under arrest for the attempted murder

of Luke Kith and Andrea Parker. You have the right to remain

silent…" Cap reads him his rights and puts him in the back

of one of the cars. He walks back to Luke and starts lecturing him.

"Jesus, Luke! Why didn't you call me before? We could have

already had him at the station! This does not look good at all!" They

hook the SUV to a tow truck and take it to the station for processing.

"I didn't think that I had enough time. I didn't want him to

get away."

"Well, I hope he doesn't press charges against you. If he

does you know you are off the case then. Not to mention that I am

going to have to suspend you! What the hell were you thinking? I

want you to go home right now. I will call you if I need you for

anything."

"Fine!" Luke says angrily and gets into his car. Just then his

phone starts to ring.

"Yeah." He answers with a pissed off attitude.

"Luke, it's me. Can you come and pick me up at the hospital?

I'm ready to go now. Matt's asleep."

"I'm on my way," and he takes off. He gets to the hospital in 15 minutes.

He goes up to the room and knocks on the door lightly before he enters. Andrea is sitting on a chair next to Matt's bed, tugging on her earlobe and looking extremely nervous. Luke bends down and whispers,

"What's wrong?"

She looks up at him and whispers back, "we'll talk on the way home." She grabs her purse and follows Luke out into the hall. Luke takes a moment to talk to Officer Mitchell, and they leave the hospital shortly after. As they get into the car, the phone rings again.

"Yeah," he answers.

"I got Reilly and his lawyer in the interrogation room. You want to join us?"

"Yeah, I will be there in ten." Luke replies, and hangs up.

"That was Cap, we need to stop at the station. Do you want to tell me why you are so upset?"

"It can wait." She isn't so sure that she wants to tell Luke about Matt and Julia and the affair. When they get to the station, Luke lets Andrea sit in his office, while he joins Cap in the interrogation room. He walks into the room, Cap turns on the recorder, and makes the introductions. *Great, Joe Higgins*, Luke thinks. *Reilly somehow manages to get the best criminal attorney in the area. The man has never lost a case.* Cap starts the questioning.

"Where were you on the morning of May 30th between noon and 1:00 p.m.?"

"I was at home."

"Was anyone with you? Can anyone verify that alibi?"

165

Captain Corrigan continues to ask.

"No, I was by myself."

"What about May 25th between midnight and 3:00a.m.?"

"I was probably at home sleeping." He says and smirks.

"Is Mr. Reilly under arrest?" Higgins interrupts.

"Yes, he is. We have reason to believe that Mr. Reilly tried to

run over the Detective here along with Dr. Andrea Parker. The lab is

working on the SUV as we speak. I am sure that we will have all the

evidence gathered within the next hour or so." Captain Corrigan

replies.

"If you dismiss these charges, we will drop the charges that

we plan to pursue with the courts. It was your detective that

assaulted Mr. Reilly in the parking lot of the grocery store. I

think that's a good deal, don't you, Captain?" Higgins asks. Captain

Corrigan thinks for a minute and then looks at Luke. Luke nods back at him.

"It's a deal."

"My client then is free to go. As far as I know, my client was sitting in a parking lot minding his own business, and your detective just picked him up for questioning. If you get anything else on my client, just give me a call." He stands up and throws his card on the table.

"We'll be in touch, Mr. Higgins. I would advise you to tell your client to stay in town."

Cap retorts back as Higgins and Reilly walk out of the room and towards the building exit.

Cap turns to Luke, "that didn't go well at all, he is definitely our man. I am going to have a tail on him and will be kept posted. I

want you to go home and take a breather. You really look like shit."
Luke laughs.

"I had a rough day! I'll go home right now." He walks to his office to get Andrea, and as approaches, he sees her rummaging through his desk. He enters the office quietly.

"Did you find anything interesting in there?" he startles her and she almost falls out of his chair.

"Gosh. Luke. You just scared the living daylights out of me!" She gets up out of the chair and straightens her skirt.

"You didn't answer my question. I asked you if you found anything interesting in my desk? I am wondering why you even went through it. You know that I don't like it when people go through my things. Not to mention, I am sure that you moved some stuff around, too. I like my shit nice and organized."

Oh, oh. Andrea tugs on her earlobe and bites her lip. *Luke is angry, really angry.* "I'm sorry," she says as apologetically as she can, "to tell you the truth, I was really bored just sitting here. You know that I can't sit still for too long."

"It's okay. I'm sorry for snapping at you. I had a really long, bad day today, and I am really tired. Let's go home." On the way home he asks, "are you hungry?"

"Not really, are you?"

"Nope. It's eleven o'clock. I want to go home and straight to bed." That is exactly what he does, and immediately notices that after Andrea uses the bathroom, that she goes straight to bed in the other room.

"Andie!" He yelled out. She got up and went to his room. He motioned for her to come over to him, and he uncovered one side of the bed so that she could lay down next to him. Andrea obeyed. She walked over to the bed, and laid down. "Do you want to talk about what's bothering you," he asked her as she got comfortable in his bed.

"No, I'm tired. I just want to go to sleep. Good night, Luke," she answered and kissed him on the lips.

"Night," he hugs her and quickly they both fall asleep.

Chapter 11

At 6:00a.m., his phone rings. "Luke," he answers.

"I want you to go to Reilly's house and take over for Bob." Cap orders. "Let me know every move he makes. He's got to be our guy. At least I hope he is. We need to find more evidence."

"I know, I will keep in touch." They hang up their phones, and Luke gets dressed. It is still too early, so he doesn't wake Andrea. He leaves her a note on his pillow that says 'call me when you wake up'. He leaves the house as Johnson pulls in into the driveway. Luke lets him know what's going on and heads out. He pulls up to Bob's car and takes over the watch so Bob can go home to rest. Knowing that Higgins probably told Reilly to be careful, Luke thinks that he is going to stay low the next few days. He takes a sip of his black coffee and waits. At about 10:00a.m., Reilly leaves the house. Luke is on his tail. He wants to make sure that Reilly

doesn't see him. After driving around for about twenty minutes,

Reilly finally pulls into a driveway. Luke pulls over on the street, a

couple of houses down. He calls Cap and gives him the address

of the house Reilly went into. A couple of minutes later, Cap calls

him back.

"Luke, the house belongs to Jeff Hughes. Don't do anything.

I repeat, do not get out of the car! Let me know when he leaves." A

half an hour later Reilly storms out of the house and sped off. Luke

calls Cap,

"You want me to follow him or do you want me to go talk to

Jeff?"

"I want you to go see Hughes first. Let me know what he has

to say. I will put an APB out on Reilly." Cap hangs up.

Luke knocks on the door and rings the doorbell. No answer.

He waits and now pounding on the door, yells out,

"This is the police. Open up Mr. Hughes. I know you're in

there!" Still, no reply.

"Cap, there's no answer, I'm going in." Luke says through his

radio. He draws his gun, and kicks the door open.

"Hughes, are you in here?" he yells as he looks around. He

makes his way through the living room, bedroom, and no sign of

him. He enters the kitchen and finds him lying, sprawled on the

floor, face up, with a knife sticking out of his chest.

"He's been stabbed," he calls on his radio while he checks

for a pulse. "I got no pulse. I repeat, I have no pulse."

"The EMT and the squad will be there soon." Cap answers

back. "I sent out an APB on Reilly, we will get him charged now."

Luke waits for his team and thinks. *Why in the world would Reilly want to kill Jeff? Was Jeff the other guy and Reilly the main suspect? How does Prochesky fit into all of this? What are we missing?*

Cap calls him, "Luke, you can come to the station. I just got word that they apprehended Reilly. They are taking him to the station as we speak."

"I will be there as soon as I can," he hangs up the phone and it rings again. "Luke," he answers.

"I got your note, so I am calling you," Andrea says.

"Hey, something just came up and I need to get to the police station now. You can have Johnson take you wherever you want to go."

"I really need to talk to you, Luke. When will I get to see you?"

"I will try to get done within the next couple of hours. I will meet you at the hospital later. Is that okay?"

"Okay, thanks. Bye"

"Bye, Andie." Luke hangs up as the team arrives to take over. He heads out of Hughes' house and to the station.

On his way to the station, he wonders what Andrea needs to talk to him about. *Apparently it's not that important.* He really needs to get to the bottom of the case first. He will worry about his relationship with Andrea later.

Luke asks as he joins Cap in his office, "Did Higgins show up yet?"

"Nope, and the damn bastard won't talk until he gets here. We got the fingerprints off the knife, and they are a match. If anything, we can nail him for the murder of Jeff Hughes. We just have to somehow get him connected with the Parkers. We have no evidence linking him to them. I hope that we can scare him into talking. I'm waiting for the prosecutor to stop by. Maybe he can make another deal with Reilly."

"Something still doesn't add up. This whole case doesn't make sense to me," Luke continues, "if Hughes and Reilly were in on it together, why kill him? The brain has got to be Hughes. Think about it. What does Reilly gain by killing him? It's not like Hughes has the flash drive. It couldn't have been pre-meditated; Reilly's fingerprints were all over the place. Someone else is involved. The Parker incident was so planned out. Nothing whatsoever was found that we could use as concrete evidence. This is one smart guy that we are looking for. Is this where Prochesky comes into the picture? Are Hughes and Reilly working for him?"

"I agree, Luke. Maybe Reilly went to the house to talk with Hughes. They argued, and Reilly stabbed him. He panicked and ran out without wiping anything down. It happens a lot with murders that are not planned."

"Yeah, well, I am starting to think that Prochesky really is behind it all. I talked with Beckman earlier today, and he said they still haven't found him," Luke says, as they are about to enter the interrogation room. The tape recorder is activated when they walk in.

"I'm not talking until my lawyer gets here," Reilly states nervously.

"Relax, we'll wait. He's on his way. He should be here shortly." After waiting a few minutes, sensing Reilly's agitation building, Cap inquires, "how did you know Jeff Hughes?"

"I don't know a Jeff Hughes," Reilly replies.

"Then why were you at his house this morning? Why are your finger prints all over the knife that killed him?"

"I don't know what you're talking about," Reilly answers right as Higgins walks in. He sits down on a seat next to Reilly, opposite Cap and Luke.

"What do we have, gentlemen?" Higgins asked.

"What we have is your client's fingerprints all over the murder weapon that we found in Jeff Hughes' body earlier this morning. We also have an eye witness that puts him at Hughes' house this morning." Cap replies and smiles. He loves being the bearer of news.

"Let me have a moment alone with my client please." Higgins states, and Cap and Luke walk out of the room.

"Can you help me out or what?" Reilly turns to Higgins.

"This is a real mess, Reilly, I don't think anyone can get you out of it. You should have wiped the knife before you left. That's your problem. I could have taken care of the witness, no problem. What were you thinking?"

"I don't know, man, I went over there to scare him, I didn't mean to kill him! You have to help me, I don't want to go to jail," Reilly pleads.

"I could say it was self-defense depending on what the witness saw. But you didn't call 911, and you ran. The jury isn't going to like that. Even if it was self-defense, they will charge you because you didn't call the police. You ran out. The police are trying to find out information about the attempted murder of Mr. Matthew Parker and the abduction of his wife, Julia. They think that you are behind it. I need to know everything that you know about the Parker incident. If we can give them something they can use, maybe we can work out some kind of a deal. If you get charged with everything and get convicted you could face the death penalty. The only way that I could try to help you is if you know something, and you speak up."

_____ * _____ * _____

Back at the hospital, Andrea walks into Matt's room and doesn't see him in the bed.

"Matt!" She yells out.

"Yes, I'm in the bathroom. I'll be right out," he calls back.

Andrea takes a seat and unpacks their lunch. Matt walks out of the bathroom and is pleasantly surprised as he takes his seat and sees a bowl of homemade chicken noodle soup.

"Wow, thanks Andrea. This hospital food is terrible, and I am starving!"

"Can I ask you something?" Knowing that it's something serious, Matt nods.

"Do you know how to trace a call?"

"Sure. All I need is the phone and my laptop."

"Just dandy," she mumbles. "The police have all of your computers. How are we going to do that?" Matt watches her pace around the room.

"Why don't you tell me what is going on, and maybe I can help you." Matt talks to her in a serene voice trying to calm her down. She looks at him for a minute and thought *what the hell*.

"I was wondering if you could trace the number from the guy

that called me. He's the one that has Julia. The police couldn't track it, so I was thinking that maybe you, Mr. Computer Genius, could do it. I really want to help Julia. The guy said that he was going to call me, but he hasn't." She sighs, "aren't you the least bit worried about Julia?"

"Honestly, no, I'm not. I tried to file for divorce two months ago. I just don't love her like I used to. She changed so much over the last three years. She isn't anything like she used to be. Besides, for some strange reason, I have a feeling that she is somehow involved in this, and I am not the only one who thinks so."

"Well, I still want to find her!"

"Okay, this is what we'll do. Call Luke and tell him to grab my laptop from the station. I don't think that he will mind. I have my notebook here, so I have the codes that I will need. You have your phone, right?"

Andrea dials Luke's number but he doesn't answer. "He

didn't answer. He's probably busy." She decides to wait a few

minutes before she calls him again.

———— * ———— * ————

In a hotel room, he watches Julia asleep on the bed. So far, he

has given them enough hints to point at her. Taking her out to dinner

was just one of them. He smirks. He knows that the NSA has been

looking for him, but he is one step ahead of them. He knows that

Reilly is getting questioned right now, and he knows that Reilly will

talk. He is just so sick of Julia. He has her thinking that he will share

the millions of dollars that he will make off of the flash drive. But now, it's time to get rid of her. He isn't going to be able to make an

exchange because the NSA has the flash drive. I don't care if Julia

lives or dies. He has been drugging her little by little the last couple

of days, and now he is ready to give her the final dose. He takes a

little bottle out of his pocket, and a syringe. He sits next to her, fills

the syringe and sticks the needle in her arm. He wipes the whole

room down, covering his tracks, picks up his bag and leaves. He

is on the move again.

Chapter 12

Luke and Cap are joined by Beckman and the county prosecutor. They spend a few minutes talking amongst themselves, before they enter the interrogation room. In no time at all, Reilly is talking. He admitted to being there that night when Matt Parker was shot. But he said that he got freaked out by it and as soon as he heard the gun shot, he ran out and left. He took off running as fast as possible getting away from the Parker home. He hitched a ride to his place. He has no idea where Julia is or what happened to her.

"Who was with you that night?" Luke asks him.

"I don't know the guy's name, but he makes me call him Einstein."

"How and when did you meet him?" Cap queries him.

"I met him about a month ago at a bar I go to a lot. He asked me if I wanted to make big bucks, and I said sure. Then he told me about this flash drive."

Then they asked him about Hughes, and what happened this morning. He said that Einstein called him and told him to meet up with Hughes to find the flash drive. Einstein gave him Hughes address.

"When I got there, Hughes said that he was going to go to the police with all of the information he had. I panicked. I didn't want to go to jail. So I saw a knife and I grabbed it. The next thing I knew we were battling. I somehow managed to stab him, and then I ran out of the house."

"How do you keep in touch with this Einstein guy?"

"I don't. He calls me. The weird part is, every time he called me, it was from a different number. This guy is totally out there. He is a real genius!" Reilly says as if he is in awe of the man.

Beckman spreads a few photos on the table. "Are any of these men Einstein?"

Reilly looks at the pictures one by one.

"Well?" Luke angrily asks.

"Yeah, this is him." He points to a picture of Prochesky.

"That is all we needed to know," Beckman says. "I think that this concludes our interrogation for now, if we need anything else, we will give Mr.Higgins a call."

"What happens to me now?" Reilly asks nervously.

"As of now, you are under arrest for the murder of Jeff Hughes. You will be processed and taken into custody." Cap gets up and exits the room, followed by Beckman and Luke.

"It looks like it's all over now." Beckman says to the two of them. "Now that we know that Prochesky is behind it all, the NSA will take over from here on out."

"But we still need to find Julia," Luke says.

"I have a feeling that Julia will show up soon. Prochesky knows that we have the flash drive. He is going to get rid of her. He no longer needs her. I will need Andrea's phone though. We need to pinpoint his location, so we will need to run the phone's memory card through our system."

"Our techs already tried it but it didn't work," Cap speaks up.

"We have better programs. You would be amazed if I told you about everything that this agency can accomplish."

Luke's cell phone rings.

"Luke," he says with an upbeat tone. He is pretty happy

about what Reilly had said.

"Hi Luke," Andrea says, and then asks "are you still at the station?"

"Yes, I am right about to leave and go to you. Did you or Matt need something?"

"Actually, yes, Matt needs the laptop that we found up in the tree house."

"Why does he need it?" Luke asks curiously.

"He said that he can trace that number off of my phone, but he needs his laptop."

"I will see what I can do. I will see you soon." He hangs up and turns to Beckman.

"That was Andrea, she wants me to bring Matt's laptop to the hospital. She said that he can trace the phone call."

189

"That sounds good to me, let's take the computer to the hospital. This way no one at the NSA will be able to give Prochesky the heads up. I still haven't figured out exactly who the mole is. Luke, you go get the laptop, and Cap, you get a team ready. As soon as we get the location I am going to call you. This time, we might just actually surprise him."

"You know, Luke, I think that you are a good detective. Would you be interested in a job with the NSA?" Beckman asks him as Luke parks his car at the hospital.

"I'm interested, what would that job entail?"

"Well you would be doing detective work, just like you are doing here. There are only two differences: You can't talk about the cases that you work on, unless you are talking with someone at NSA. You can tell others that you work for us. But that is all. You would be doing some traveling, depending on the cases. You interested?"

"I will let you know," Luke smiles. He wants to talk with Andrea about it first.

They knock on Matt's door and enter the hospital room, where Matthew and Andrea are waiting patiently.

"We have the laptop, is there anything else you need, Matt?" Beckman asks.

"Nope, I have Andrea's phone right here," he holds it up so everyone can see it. Luke and Beckman grab a seat and watch Matthew get to work.

He takes the battery out of Andrea's phone and then a little memory card. He loads the memory card into the laptop and waits. "It will take a couple of minutes for the memory card to load on to the computer. Andrea, you need a new phone. You are way behind

191

on technology."

She turns red out of embarrassment.

"I know, how about you take me phone shopping when you are well?"

"That sounds like a promise that I will hold you to," he says to her as he pulls the memory card back out of the laptop, and inserts it into her phone. He looks in his little notebook and types in a bunch of codes and commands. They all stand around the computer and watch.

"Wow," Luke says as a huge map of the world comes on the screen. Matt types in the phone number and some kind of command. In a matter of seconds another map pops up on the screen. A big red star shows up and next to it is an address: 4502 Huntington Drive.

"Here it is, boys, make sure you write it down." Matt proudly says.

Beckman gets on his cell, "We got an address. It's 4502 Huntington Drive. When can your team meet us there?"

"We can be there in twenty minutes." Cap replies.

"Perfect. But don't do anything until you hear from me again." He hangs up.

"Matt, can you look up the building plans of the address? I want to devise our plan before we get there.

"Sure, no problem." He looks it up and shows Beckman the place. It is Holiday Inn. There are five entrances and exits to the hotel. Five floors, and there are 200 rooms total.

Beckman gets on his phone again. "Patton, I need you to see if any of Prochesky's aliases have been used to check in at the Holiday Inn at 4502 Huntington Drive. Also check under Julia

Parker. Call me back right away. Thanks."

He hangs up and then calls Cap. "Don't go anywhere just yet. Luke and I will meet you at the station first."

On the way to the station, Patton called Beckman and told him that Prochesky was checked into room number 302. As far as they knew, he should still be there. According to the desk, Prochesky hadn't check out yet. Beckman informed Luke and as soon as they got to the station, plans of the hotel were sprawled on Cap's desk.

"I figure we cover all of the exits, and do a thorough search of the place. Have your men dress undercover, I don't want to draw any attention to the place, and I don't want Prochesky to know that we are on to him. Not to mention, as far as we know, he has Julia. I don't want her to get hurt. This pretty much covers it all. Let's go and get started," Beckman orders.

"I am having the officers gather in the conference room. As soon as we get the plan out, we will head out," Cap states.

In the conference room, everyone received a photo of Prochesky and their instructions. Cap designated a spot for every officer involved, and they left in groups of three. They headed out in their own cars, in street clothes. Once they arrived at the hotel, they all followed their orders.

_____ * _____ * _____

Andrea looks at Matt. "What are you thinking?"

"I was thinking of how stupid I am. I should have had that private investigator keep tailing her. I wish I could go home and look through all of those addresses he gave me. I want to see if she went to that hotel before. I have a feeling that she is in on all of this. Do

you think that I could get released tonight?" He looks at her and

pouts. "You are a doctor, and you will be with me at all times." He

pleads to her. "Please, Andrea!"

"I'll tell you what, you rest while I will go have a little chat

with Dr. Newman, and we will see what she thinks. But, no

promises." She smiles at him and leaves the room in search

of Dr. Newman. An hour later, she came back into the room with

discharge papers in hand. "All you have to do is sign these papers,

and then we can go. I went home and brought you a shirt and

a pair of sweats that you can change into." She hands him the bag.

"You are the best! Thank you!" he moves off the bed and

yelps. Andrea gives him a dirty look.

"You need to be careful!" she tells at him. "We are going to have to stop at the drugstore before we go home. We need to pick up your prescriptions, and some dressings. Dr. Newman has already scheduled you an appointment with her in one week." Matt goes into the bathroom to change. Ten minutes later, he and Andrea exit the room with Matthew seated in a wheelchair.

"You guys ready to go?" Officer Johnson, who was in charge of watching Matt asks.

"Yes, we are. We will need to stop at the pharmacy though. I need to pick up his medicine."

"That won't be a problem," Officer Johnson carefully leads them outside of the hospital and into the vehicle. As they leave, he calls Luke. "Just wanted to let you know that Mr. Parker was released from the hospital. We are on the way back to the house."

"Okay. We are getting ready to enter the hotel now. Make

sure you keep a good look out, we aren't sure where Prochesky is."

Luke hangs up, and with Cap and Beckman, they enter the hotel. He looks around making sure that the officers he sees are where they should be. They get into the elevator and he presses floor number 3. When they reach the floor, they step out and casually walk over to room number 302. Three raps to the door.

"Room service," Beckman calls out. They wait a minute and no one answers the door. Once again he knocks on the door. "Room service," he yells out louder, but still no one comes to the door. Beckman looks at them and nods. He takes a key card out and swipes it. The door unlocks and slowly he opens it. First, they walk through a little hallway. Beckman goes straight and heads into a little living room. All empty. Luke walks up to a partly opened door on the left. He pushes the door with his leg, and enters with his gun in hand. He spots Julia lying on the bed and a phone on the nightstand. He looks around and makes sure that no one else is in the room and calls out.

"I have Julia!" He runs over to her and checks her pulse. "I have no pulse." He looks at the other two. Cap gets on the phone and calls it in.

"The CSI and the coroner are on their way. They will be here in ten." Cap notifies the other officers through his radio and shuts down the hotel. He wants to check every room in the hotel. Prochesky hasn't been spotted, and Beckman doesn't think that he left the hotel. Unless, they were too late.

After a few hours, having checked out the whole hotel, they realize that they missed Prochesky, again. The coroner gave the time of death for Julia, but that's all he could do. The body was taken to the coroner's lab for an autopsy. The room was dusted for prints, and

none were found at the scene. Luke disappointedly turns to Beckman

and asks,

"So now what?"

"Now, it's over. Prochesky is probably out of the country.

We were just too late. We have Reilly in custody, Matthew is going

to be fine, the flash drive is safe for the time being, and we just

found Julia dead. There is nothing else that you can do. I will be

searching for Prochesky and I won't stop until I get him. You are

more than welcome to join me and my team." He shakes Luke's

hand, as well as Cap's, and leaves the hotel.

Chapter 13

At the drugstore, having left Matt in the car with Officer Johnson, Andrea is waiting for the prescriptions to be filled. As she waits, she browses around the store. She picks up a bottle of her favorite shampoo, a new toothbrush and a bottle of body wash. All of her stuff is at Luke's. When the medicine is ready, she pays for everything and walks out of the store. She puts the bags in the trunk and gets in the car.

"Did you get everything?" Matt asks her.

"Yup! Maybe I can stop at the grocery store now, too. I want to make us dinner," she says as they near Giant Eagle.

"No, I want to go home. You can drop me off there, and then go grocery shopping. I think I need to lie down, I'm getting pretty sleepy, and I feel as if all my energy has drained out."

Andrea nods as they pass the store. Once they get home, she gets

Matt situated in a spare bedroom on the first floor. She gave him the

medicine that he needed to take, and he dozed right off. The room is

right next to a main floor bathroom, so it is a perfect set up. She

figures that she will sleep on one of the couches in the living room,

close enough to hear him, and that she will take care of him until he

is well enough to manage on his own.

She put on a pot of coffee, and wrote down on a piece of

paper all the things she will need from the grocery store. She feels

like making meatloaf with mashed potatoes, and gravy, with a salad.

She pours a cup of coffee and takes it out to Johnson who was

parked in the driveway. She told him that Matt was sleeping in the

bedroom downstairs. She returns to her list and calls the local grocery store and asks if they could deliver what she needs. For a small fee, they promised her delivery will arrive within the hour. She's content and feels that she will have plenty of time to make dinner and dessert.

About 45 minutes later, the groceries arrive and she puts them on the kitchen counter. Walking to the bedroom to check on Matt, she hears the phone ring but is intent on checking in on him, so she ignores the call. *Oh, he's sleeping like a baby. He is resting comfortably, what more could I ask for?* She glances at her watch and sees that it is 4:30 pm. She figures that she better start dinner right now, so that it's ready by 7:00pm. On a mission, she forgets all about her phone.

He called her three times and she didn't answer. He is pretty pissed off at her now. He had to call Johnson to check up on the two of them. He sat in his car and dialed her number again. The phone rings twice and…

"Hello," she answers.

"Finally! I have been trying to get a hold of you!" Luke irritably exclaims.

"Sorry, Luke. I have been busy. I have been making dinner for all of us."

"I have some news, but I will let you guys in on everything when I get there. I will be there soon. Do you need me to bring you anything?"

"No thanks, just yourself. I shall see you soon then. Bye."

She hangs up. *I wonder what news he has for us. He sounded "odd" on the phone and I have no idea if he is mad at me for not answering the phone, or if it has something to do with the case.* She slides the meatloaf in the oven and starts to peel the potatoes. After

they are cooking on the stove, she makes the dessert – a no-bake

easy éclair dessert. She found the recipe in one of her cookbooks

back at home, easy to remember, easy to make and tastes great. She

assembled and refrigerated the dessert and then went in to check on

Matt. He was still sleeping. She has about one more hour before

everything is done, so she decided to wait a little longer before

waking him up.

She went to the dining room and set the table. She put four

settings on the table planning on Officer Johnson joining them. She

stepped outside to let him know that dinner will be ready in twenty

minutes, and to make sure that he comes in. After the table was set

exactly as she wanted, she went to Matt's room to wake him.

"Matt," she whispers, "it's time to wake up."

"Is it time for dinner yet? I am starving!"

"It will be ready soon. Luke is on his way and he said that he has some news for us."

"Really?" Matt asks intrigued. "Did he say what?"

"No, he said that he will discuss everything with us when he gets here."

With that said, Matthew gets out of bed and goes to the bathroom.

"I will be in the kitchen!" she yells out to him.

A few minutes later, the doorbell rings. She runs out of the kitchen and opens up the door expecting Luke, instead it was Officer Johnson.

"Please come in," Andrea says, and Officer Johnson comes in and closes the door behind him. "Why don't you have a seat in the dining room, Matt is probably in there. I will go to the kitchen and finish everything up. Just go straight down the hallway, and make a

left. If you need to wash up the bathroom is right there." She points

to it.

"Yes, ma'am. Thank you for inviting me. It has been a while

since I had a homemade meal." The doorbell rings again. "I will get

it," he says as Andrea rushes off to the kitchen. He looks through the

peephole and sees Luke standing there. He opens it up and Luke

comes in, "How's it going, Luke?" Officer Johnson asks.

"I had a pretty shitty day. I will tell you about it over dinner.

But I do have some good news, too, that you will be happy about. Is

Andrea in the kitchen?"

"Yes, and Matt's in the dining room. I'm headed to the

bathroom, I need to wash up. Don't start to talk about anything until

I get there. I want to know everything you know." He winks at Luke and goes into the bathroom, while Luke heads to the kitchen.

"Hey," he says to her as he walks in.

"Hi." She studies him. He must have gone home and changed she thought. He was wearing a black pair of jeans and a white t-shirt that was tucked in his pants. Instead of tennis shoes that he was wearing this morning, now he had on a pair of black loafers. *He is so sexy*. The look on his face was not what she expected to see. Instead of being happy to see her, he looked sad and troubled.

"Do you need any help?"

"Sure," she points to the counter, "what's wrong?"

"I will tell you everything when we all sit." He picks up the salad bowl in one hand and the bread basket in the other. Andrea takes the meatloaf out of the oven and they carry it all to the dining room where they set it on the table. Luke greeted Matthew and sat down opposite him, next to Officer Johnson. Andrea went back to the kitchen to retrieve the mashed potatoes and the gravy. As soon as she put everything down, she sat right next to Matthew, opposite Officer Johnson. Matthew spoke up,

"Well, Luke? I can tell the news that you have for us isn't good, so just tell us what's going on."

"We found Julia at the hotel today, but we were late. She was dead when we got there. I'm really sorry." He looks at Matthew, and then at Andrea. Her eyes start to water and she hugs Matthew and tells him how truly sorry she is.

"It's okay, Andrea." She squeezes him a little and he grabs her hands and moves her body back to her seat. She was hurting him. With no expression on his face, he looks at Luke and asks,"Who killed her, do you know?"

"We think it's Prochesky. As a matter of fact, we think that

he was behind all of it. That's what all the evidence points to. We are

closing the case. Beckman thinks that Prochesky is already gone."

"How did she die?" Andrea interrupts Luke.

"We don't know yet, the coroner will have a final report by

tomorrow morning." They begin eating the meal laid out in front of

them and Luke says, "as of tomorrow, Johnson, you will be getting a

new assignment. But Cap wants you to stick around here tonight,

just in case."

"No problem, Maddox will actually be here around ten to

take over the watch." Trying to make light of the situation Officer

Johnson says, "this is a really great meal, Miss Parker. Thank

you again, for inviting me." He quickly cleans his plate, and stands

up. "I will be outside if anyone needs me." He leaves and goes back to his car parked right in front of the house.

"Now what?" Andrea asks Luke as finishes his food.

"Nothing, there is nothing that we can do."

"What about Julia's body?" inquires Matt.

"That will be released to you as soon as the coroner makes

his report. How are you doing so far?'

"I don't know. I still need time to process everything. To tell

you the truth, I can't believe that Julia's dead. I was a hundred

percent sure that she was behind all of it."

"I know, again, I am so sorry. I wish that we had made it to

the hotel earlier today. As for knowing what she had to do with any

of this, I guess we'll never know." Luke slides his empty plate over,

and looks at Andrea.

"You aren't going to eat?" Andrea hadn't even put anything

on hers yet.

"No, I'm not really hungry," she wipes her eyes with a napkin, and starts to clear the table. "I made something for dessert, does anyone want a piece?"

"No thanks," Matt and Luke say in unison.

"I, however, would love a cup of coffee," adds Matt. Andrea nods and gives him a little smile as she walks into the kitchen. She poured them each a cup of coffee and when she brought it into the dining room. No one was there. She put the serving tray with the coffee on the table and went to find them. She went to the living room and found it empty. She called out to them, and there was no answer. Andrea started to panic. *Where are they?* She runs out to Officer Johnson who was sitting in the car.

"I can't find them!" she says excitedly and Johnson gets out of the car.

"What do you mean?"

"I went into the kitchen to make coffee and when I came back, there was nobody there. I looked everywhere downstairs, and I called out to them but no one answered."

"Come on," he said to her, "stand right behind me." He walks them over to the front door. "Be very quiet," he whispers to her as he slowly walks into the house, with her right behind him. She was so close to Officer Johnson, that when he stopped, she ran right into him. He turns back to her, and puts his index finger to his lips. He checks all of the rooms downstairs and didn't find anyone. He goes up the stairs and then checks all of the rooms, and still no one.

"There is no one here!" he says surprised, and he leads her back downstairs and into the kitchen. "I am going to call Luke." He

213

pulls out his phone and dials. Luke answers.

"Luke."

"Where in the hell are you? Andrea and I just searched the whole damn house, and no one is in it!" he yells at him.

"Relax, Johnson! Matt wanted to get some fresh air, we are in the back, near the tree house. I was just about to go in and check to see what was taking Andrea so long with the coffee, so we could have it out on the patio."

"You scared the crap out of both of us, I'll have you know!" he hangs up the phone. He tells Andrea that they are both outside near the treehouse and will meet her on the patio, and then goes back to his car. Andrea takes the tray with the coffee outside through the dining room door to the patio. She is fuming! And yet, she felt stupid for not checking the backyard. She must apologize to Officer Johnson. She is so embarrassed. She put the tray on the table and with hands on her hips she yells at the two of them as they approach.

"What is wrong with the two of you? One of you could have let me know that you would be out here. I was totally freaked out. I had no idea where you were. Didn't you hear me call your names? I had to go and get poor Officer Johnson to help me look for you!"

"Sorry, Andrea," Matthew says as he reaches for a coffee cup and adds the sugar and cream to it. "I just wanted to grab some fresh air, stretch my legs, and I guess we were deep in conversation."

"It's okay," she answers, but gives Luke a dirty look. She takes a seat and takes her cup of coffee, as well. "Do you want some, Luke?"

"No thanks, I will be leaving soon. I need to still go check some stuff out at the station and then I am going to go home."

"Oh," Andrea says disappointed. She was hoping that Luke was going to stay a while. She wondered what was going to happen to the two of them now that the case is closed. She really wants to talk to him. "Do you really have to go? I was hoping that you can hang out here for a while."

"I'll tell you what. I will go to the station and when I am done there, I will come back here." He looks at his watch. It's almost nine. Are you guys going to stay out here a while longer? If you are I will send Johnson over here to watch over you."

"No," Matthew replies, "just give me a few more minutes, Luke, and then I will go in." He finishes his coffee and gets up. "I am going to take my medicine and go to bed. Thanks for everything, Luke." He shakes Luke's hand. Luke and Andrea clear the table and she brings in the tray.

"I will see you later then," Luke tells Andrea as he puts his

lips on hers for a quick kiss. "I will be back."

"Surprised by his distant actions tonight, she just nods at him,

as she watches him leave her in the kitchen, all alone.

Chapter 14

He gets in the car and speeds off. Luke is overwhelmed with

all of the feelings and stress that he has been having the last week.

They managed to close the case, but now he has bigger problems to

worry about. Ever since Beckman offered him a job, he has thought

about accepting the offer. He still wanted to find Prochesky. If he

takes the job, it would mean that he wouldn't see Andrea as often. If

he proposes to her again, she might again, say no. He has no idea

where their relationship is heading and what Andrea wants out of it.

He has no idea what she plans on doing now. His goal tonight is

finding that out. But right now, he wants to go to the station,

check the coroner's report, and then put in his letter of resignation.

No matter how his conversation ends up with Andrea, he will still take this job, no matter what. His relationship with Andrea will have to play out with him taking the job. To Luke the case is still not closed. It won't be closed until Prochesky is found and behind bars.

Back at the station, he goes into Cap's office, and luckily, he is still there, wrapping up the report.

"I'm surprised to see you back tonight," Cap comments.

"I came back to see the coroner's report and I wanted to talk to you about something."

"I am all ears! What's on your mind, Luke?"

"Do you remember how I told you about the job offer that Beckman offered?"

"Yes, I do. Have you decided?"

"I will accept it. I wanted you to be the first to know. I will hand in my letter of resignation to the human resources department tomorrow."

"Good for you, Luke!" Cap says proudly. "I couldn't be any happier for you! We will all surely miss you."

"You'll see me. I will be working right here in Colorado, unless I need to travel depending on the case that I get. We will still get together for drinks."

"I know we will, but things will be so different without you. It's going to take a while to get used to not calling you to my office." Cap laughs. "What about Andrea?"

"What about her?"

"Come on, Luke, spit it out. I know how you feel about her."

"That's where things get a little complicated. I don't know what's going to happen with us," Luke replies as he stands up. "Speaking of which, I wanted to go there tonight to talk to her.

Right now, I will write up my resignation and review the coroner's report. I need to call Agent Beckman to let him know, that as of tomorrow, I have handed in my resignation and I will be joining his team. Good night, Cap."

"Good night, Luke."

Later, on the way to the Parker residence, Luke thinks about how he will tell Andrea about the new job. He started to think about that night when he proposed. They were both out of college and they both had plans to do what each of them wanted. *I knew that Andrea planned on going to MED school in Seattle, and she knew that I was going to start a job as a police officer here in Colorado. I asked her to marry me, because I wanted her to stay here, and now that I think about it, I told her quite a few times that she should stay here, after she finished college. This is why I proposed. My God! I understand now why she said no. It finally makes sense to me.*

She must have thought that if she said yes that I would have made

her stay here, and not go on to become a doctor. Not once, did I give

her a hint that I was willing to go there. Back then, I don't think that

I was willing to go and she knew that. She was accepted to one of the

best MED schools in the country. I was selfish, I should have never

asked her to make such a decision. But I did, and she picked the

school. It didn't mean that she didn't love me. To think, I didn't give

her a chance to explain. I love her, and I don't want to lose her

again. I wonder if we could make a long distance relationship work.

I wonder if just maybe, I should sacrifice for her. It's not like we

have to get married right away. Maybe we will come up with

something together when we have our talk tonight.

Luke pulls up in the driveway and exits his car. He walks up to the police car and greets Officer Maddox, who took over for

Johnson for the night. He then heads up to the front door and rings

the bell. After a couple of minutes, Andrea opens the door.

"Hi, please come in. Would you like a cup of coffee or

anything else to drink? I started a pot a few minutes ago, it should be

just about ready." He follows her to the kitchen.

"Coffee sounds good, thanks." He takes a seat at the little

breakfast table, and waits for Andrea to join him. She pours them

each a cup of coffee and sits down at the table across from him.

"So what would you like to talk about?" she asks Luke.

"I decided to take a job with the NSA."

"Wow, that's wonderful," she smiles at him.

"Yeah, I am pretty excited about it. I will be working here, at

their headquarters, but it will involve some traveling. What I really want to talk to you about is us." Luke swallows and Andrea's heart starts to beat faster.

"What about us?"

"Andie," he grabs her hand and holds it, "I love you, and I am thrilled that you showed up back in my life. But I don't know what it is that you want. How do you see our future?"

"Luke, what do you want?"

"I want us to be together forever, just like I did years ago. I only realized tonight why you said no, and I am sorry for being so selfish and stubborn."

"I'm sorry, too. I'm sorry that I said no. I want to spend the rest of my life with you, too." He leans over and kisses her.

"Does this mean that you would marry me if I asked?"

"Yes," she smiles, "are you asking?"

"Maybe. We need to talk about what would happen then?"

"Luke, I have done what I wanted to do. I became a doctor and I love my job. I realized, since I have been here, that home is where the heart is, and my heart is where you are. I can move back to Colorado and get a job here. Matt needs me now, too."

Luke moves from his seat to one bended knee and asks,

"Well then, Andrea Parker, will you marry me? I don't have a ring yet, but we can pick one out together."

"Yes, I will marry you!" She kisses him and then backs away. "What did you do with the other ring?"

"I still have it," he replies as he stands.

"Well then, that's the ring I want to have. I want to show you exactly how much I love you. I want to show you exactly how happy, you just made me feel." She leads him to her bedroom.

Chapter 15

What is going on in there? He had parked his car down the street and has been looking at the house through his binoculars for the last couple of hours. He wonders why there was a cop still there when he knows that they closed the case. He also knows that the NSA thinks he had left the country. Out of boredom, he thinks about the late night rendezvous he had. *Man, I never expected what a time I would have with that woman! She rocked my world. Such animal aggressiveness. She took me to heights I never expected. She maneuvered me how she wanted it. I lost control of myself, and she had me in the palm of her hand. As soon as I opened the door to the hotel room, she kissed me hard. She pushed me against the door, pulled down my pants and grabbed my already hard dick. I had to push her away, I didn't want to come yet. I took off all of her clothes, and leaned her over the sofa. Oh, God, she felt so good.*

I thrust hard into her from behind, and she screamed. A couple of

more, slow, hard thrusts, and then I let her have it hard and fast just

like how she wanted it. Too bad I won't be staying around for more

of her, but I have an agenda I must follow through on. Maybe at a

later date we can catch up and see what she has in store for me. I

never planned on it to go like it did. I just thought that I would use

her to get information about Parker.

Julia was nothing like her. She only wanted me to get back at

her husband, and to share in what I would get from him. She didn't

turn me on at all, she thought her connection to Matthew was a turn

on for me. Then in Seattle, I sure never got a rise out of Andrea. She

had no intention of letting me into her life, let alone her bed. But

imagine if I had, I could have had her then, and now her brother,

Matt, my hostage. He sees that the front door of the house opens and

that the one man who has been there the last hour or so leaves.

Thank God! Now he will wait about ten more minutes before going

into the house.

After Luke leaves, Andrea checks on Matt and then lies

down on the couch in the living room. She put her head on a throw

pillow and covered herself with the blanket that she brought

downstairs with her. It doesn't take her long to fall asleep. She had

an emotionally exhausting day.

All of a sudden, Matt hears the front door open. *Maybe*

Andrea went somewhere with Luke and then came back, he thinks to

himself as he hears footsteps going to the upstairs, or maybe he's

dreaming. He closes his eyes and falls back to sleep. A few minutes

later, the bedroom door opens and a man with a gun, dragging

Andrea, laden with clothes, into the room. Matt's eyes open, and he sees the man who tried to kill him a little over a week ago.

"Get up!"

"Oh dear God," is all she could murmur.

"Do as I say, and I won't hurt you. Get up and let's go." Matt gets up and Prochesky nudges him. Matt flinches as he feels the pain.

"Get dressed," he takes a pair of black slacks from Andrea and throws it on the bed with a light blue dress shirt. Matthew dresses as fast as his body permits him.

"Hurry up, Mr.Parker, we need to go!"

"The police have the flash drive," Andrea intervenes.

"I know where the drive is," Prochesky smirks. "Come on," he grabs Matthew and pushes him a step ahead of him, while he held on to Andrea.

"Where are we going?" asks Matt.

"You will find out sooner or later. Right now we are going to get rid of your sister."

"Don't you dare hurt her!" Matt yells, "If you do, I won't help you. If she goes than I go."

"Ugh," Prochesky rolls his eyes. "I figured that you might say that, so I won't hurt her. I do need to make sure that she is unable to get to a phone." He leads them to the kitchen and tells Andrea to grab a chair. He then makes them walk to the living room, and has Andrea put the chair in the middle of the room. "Sit," he orders and she obeys. He throws his knapsack at Matt's feet and orders him to pull a rope out of it. He has Matthew tie her feet together and to the chair, and then her hands together behind her back. Prochesky checks the ties and then just to make sure, he has

Matt tie the rope all around her. He grabs tape and slaps a piece over

her mouth and around her head. "We are almost ready to go."

"Where exactly are we going?" Matthew asks.

"How stupid do you think that I am? Let's go." He pushes

Matthew ahead. He has everything ready. He has the two plane

tickets and the fake passports in the car. They walk past the police

car and Matthew looks in it, *Damn it! He killed him!!!* Prochesky

gets Matthew in his car and handcuffs him to the inside door handle.

He then walks over to the driver's side and takes the seat behind the

wheel.

"What do you need me for?" Matthew asks.

"Because I can't have the flash drive, I am going to get you

to show me everything that goes on it. You are going to give me the sets of codes that I need."

"What makes you think that I will?"

"If you don't, I will kill Andrea just like I did your beautiful

wife." He laughs. "You do want your sister to live, don't you?"

Matthew nods. "All you have to do is help me make the program.

After I have that, I will let you go. But one false move, and I will

have a hit on Andrea. Understood?"

"Yes, I understand."

Prochesky parks the car at the airport. He takes the plane

tickets and the passports out of the glove compartment.

"Don't think about doing anything stupid, Matthew." He

leans over and unlocks the handcuffs. "All I have to do is press

number 1 on my phone, and Andrea dies." They both get out

of the car and walk into the airport.

Chapter 16

Back at the house, Andrea tries to think of how she can get herself out of this situation and on the phone. *How come Officer Maddox didn't see anything? They left through the front door. Oh, my God! He probably hurt him! Come on Andrea, think, think, think!* She tries to move the chair and tries to undo her hands. She was able to slide the chair because of the wooden floor. She makes it to the kitchen entrance and looks around. The phone is on the wall at the opposite end. Sitting down, she won't be able to reach it. She needs to get her hands loose. She slides across the kitchen and as soon as she has neared herself to the wall with the phone, she loses her balance and falls to the side. *Damn it!* She wiggles and wiggles. She managed to loosen the rope that was tied all around her. She wiggles and moves. She needs to figure a way of getting the chair up. She

can't get the rope off. She lies there, on the kitchen floor, tied to a

chair and she feels helpless and locked away from the world.

_____ * _____ * _____

Luke has been lying in bed ever since he came back from

Andrea's. But he couldn't fall asleep. There was something still that

he felt was wrong. He kept thinking about Prochesky. Beckman told

him earlier that Prochesky was on a flight to France. But Luke had

this bad feeling as if this whole thing just wasn't over yet. Luke

couldn't accept the fact that Prochesky gave up and left. He looks at

the alarm clock and it is 1:30 am. He told Beckman that he would

meet him in the morning at the NSA headquarters. He really needs to get some rest. He closes his eyes and falls asleep.

His cell phone rings,

"Luke."

"It's Cap, where are you?"

"I'm at home trying to sleep, why? What's going on?" Luke

sits up at the side of his bed. He looks at the clock, it is 5 am.

"I can't get a hold of Maddox. He isn't answering his cell."

"He was there when I left. I doubt he left his post. Maybe

something happened. I will go and check it out. I will call you when

I get there." Luke hangs up, and quickly pulls on a pair of jeans and

a black t-shirt. He gets into his car, puts his lights on, and speeds off

to the Parker residence. He turned off the lights at the beginning of

the street and proceeds to the house. He parks his car right next to

Maddox's, gets out, and walks over to it. He sees that someone is in there, he calls out, "Maddox". He doesn't move. Luke opens the

door and flashes his light around. "Maddox!" he shakes him. Seeing

then, a bullet wound to the chest. He checks the pulse at the neck.

Nothing. *Shit!* He takes his phone out and dials Cap,

"I'm at the house. Maddox is dead in his car. The lights are

all off in the house, and I have no idea if anyone is in there."

"I'll send backup, don't go in alone!" Cap orders.

"I can't wait, Cap, I'm sorry, I'm going in." Luke hangs up.

"Luke! Luke! Damn it!" Cap gets up and runs out of the

office to the control center. "Officer down, Maddox has been shot,

send out all units to the Parker address. Baily!" he calls out, as he

sees her enter the station. She runs over to him. "You are coming

with me." They walk out to his car and drive off.

Luke takes his gun out of the holster and carefully crept up to the front door. He checks the knob and it's locked. *Damn it!* He

sticks his hand in his pocket and gets a little black, zippered case out.

He opens it up and takes out a lock pick. He jimmies it in the lock

until he hears a little click that opens the door, and steps inside. With

a flashlight in one hand and his gun in the other, he moves first

towards the room where Matt was sleeping. He opens it and sees

nothing. He closes the door and then checks the living room. He

hears a noise coming from the kitchen and carefully walks up to the

entrance. He turns the lights on and sees Andrea tied to a chair lying

on the floor. He runs over to her. He removes the tape from her

mouth.

"Ouch! He has Matt." She blurts out.

"Are they here?" he unties the ropes and sets her free. She

reaches to Luke to pull herself up on her feet.

"No, he took him somewhere. You have to find him, Luke!"

she pleads as the police start swarming in.

"Tell me everything that happened," he says to her as Cap

comes over to them.

"I was sleeping on the couch when he came in."

"Do you know who?" Luke interrupts.

"Yes, it's that man, Eric Powers, Prochesky! He woke me

pointing a gun at me. He took me to Matt's bedroom upstairs to get

fresh clothes for Matt. Then he had me lead him to the room where

Matt was sleeping. There, he told Matt to get dressed and that if he

didn't listen, that he would shoot me." She takes in a breath and

exhales.

"Then what?" asks Cap.

"Then Matt and he tied me up, and they left. I don't know

where they were going!"

"What time did this happen?"

"I don't know, but I know I fell asleep on the kitchen floor."

After she gave all of the information that she had, she started to cry.

"Luke, call Beckman and fill him in. I am going to re-issue an APB and alert all of the bus stations, the train station, and the airports. I want everyone on the lookout. They may be long gone, but we can't take a chance. We have to get Prochesky." They each get on their phones and start calling. Baily comes over to Andrea and tries to console her.

"They will find him," Baily grabs her hand and offers her a chair at the breakfast table. "Do you want me to make some coffee?"

"You don't have to do that," Andrea politely answers.

"It's really not any trouble, and to tell you the truth, I could use a cup." Baily smiled at her and walked over to the coffee pot. Luckily, everything that she needed for the coffee was right in the cabinet above the coffee pot. The coffee was going to be done in no time. She turns around and comes face to face with Luke.

"Baily, I need a favor." He looks over at Andrea who was sitting at the breakfast table.

"What do you need for me to do?"

"I need you to watch Andrea. Beckman is meeting me here soon, and I am going to leave. I don't want her to be here alone."

"She won't be alone, Luke! I'm sure that Cap will make sure that someone is to watch over her."

"Yes, he is, and we both decided that you are going to be the one."

"Come on, I'm not a babysitter!"

"Look, Baily, out of everyone at the station, other than Cap, you are the only one I trust. Please don't give me a hard time about it."

"Fine, but that means you keep me in the loop. You got it?" She rolls her eyes and taps him with her index finger on his chest.

"Thank you," he looks at Andrea and sighs.

"Don't worry about her Luke, she will be just fine. I will be with her 24/7, okay?"

"I know, Baily, this is why I am so glad that you are doing this for me. You have no idea how much I appreciate it." As he walks over to Andrea, who was sitting at the breakfast table, his phone rings.

"Luke," he answers.

"It's Beckman. They were spotted at the airport, we need to go right away. I have two of my men watching them. I will be at the house, in ten minutes. Wait for me outside." He hangs up.

"Andie," he says to her as he comes over and takes a seat. She looks at him teary-eyed. "I need to go. They have been spotted at the airport." Andrea just continues to look at him. "Officer Baily is going to be with you at all times. You will need to listen to her and behave. By that, I mean, do not go anywhere without her by your side. Prochesky has your brother, and he is most likely using you to keep Matthew doing what he wants him to do." Andrea nods as tears stream down her face.

"Please find him. I don't know what I would do without him. He is the only family I have Left, Luke. I, I, I don't..." Luke leans over squeezing her in a hug and plants a kiss on her cheek.

"It will all be okay," he consoles her. "I will find him, and bring him back in one piece, I promise," he holds her face in his palms and looks into her eyes "I promise, Andie." He leans in and gently kisses her again. He hears a car horn, and let go of her. "I need to go, I will call you, okay?" he wipes her tears and stands up. She quickly gets up and hugs him tight. She didn't want him to leave her. He embraces her back and then kisses her quickly on the lips. "Bye, Andie. Don't forget, listen to Baily, and I will call you." Baily watches the scene play out in the kitchen between Andrea and Luke. She now knows that she doesn't have a chance with Luke, Andrea won him. He runs out of the house and waves to Cap as he gets into Beckman's car.

"I told you to meet me outside!" Beckman says irritably as he pulls out of the driveway, and starts to speed to the airport. "They are getting on a flight headed to Paris, France. Two of my men are going to get on the flight with them. We are going to take a private jet and meet in Paris."

"Why don't they just arrest him right now? Why the wait?" Luke questions.

"Prochesky is a spy. I have worked with him for years. I know how he thinks. He is very dangerous and he will shoot to kill. I am sure that he has dangerous devices on him."

"Devices? Like what? Hasn't the security picked up on them? He can't possibly be carrying a gun!"

"TSA can't detect all of the devices. One example, is a pen that is actually a bomb. All he has to do is click it to activate it. This pen alone can take down the whole section of the airport that he is standing in. I can't touch him until he is all alone somewhere. We can't put innocent lives in danger. There are many other such devices that he can use that could cause a lot of damage. I have a catalog in my briefcase that I will give to you that will show you everything that we have, that he probably has, and everything that these devices can do." He gets on his cell and calls someone.

"What's the update?"…… "Okay, we are almost there. Is the plane ready?"…. "See you shortly." He hangs up, and turns to Luke.

"They are both on the flight to Paris. The flight departed 10 minutes ago. I hope that we can get there before he does."

"Don't we have a connection to someone there?" Luke asks.

"We do, and I will call him from the plane." Beckman parks the car in the back of the airport, by a private jet terminal. When they exit the car, they approach two men and a couple of security guards who were waiting. Beckman, Luke and the two men enter the plane as the two security officers stay behind. Beckman opens up the cockpit and lets the pilot know that they are ready for takeoff.

As they get seated Beckman makes the introductions.

"Gentlemen," he turns to the two men that Luke hasn't met. "This is Luke Kith. He is the newest member to our team. Luke, meet Agent Lowes," he points to a man with dark hair, and brown eyes. He is in his mid- forties and is shorter than Luke by about an inch. He was dressed in a black suit and tie. Luke shakes his hand.

"This guy over here," he says to Luke, is Agent Morrow." Agent Morrow is the complete opposite of Agent Lowes. Morrow is 6' 4" tall and has blond hair and blue eyes, and he looks much younger than all of them. Beckman puts his briefcase on the table that is between them all, and takes out a few folders, a small laptop, a few gadgets, and a catalog. He passes each one of them a manila folder with their names on it.

"In the folder, you will see all of the information about Prochesky. In it are his picture, a list of all of the aliases that he has used that we are aware of, and addresses of homes that he has all over the world."

Luke opens up the folder and looks at everything. Prochesky has ten different names that he uses, and he has a cottage outside of Paris. He has a place in California, a place in Italy, and one in Russia.

"So what's our plan, Beckman?" Agent Morrow asks.

"I don't want to do anything at the airport. I want you two to tail him," he points to Morrow and Lowes. "Luke and I are going to set up shop near his cottage." He takes a map out of the briefcase and spreads it on the table. "This is where his cottage is." He circles

the point in red. "He could be taking Mr. Parker there. However,

Prochesky has been known to suspect what we may think he would

do, so I think that he will be taking him somewhere else. He knows

that we know of this address. This is why it is extremely important

that we don't lose them, once they get off of the plane. Luke and I

are going to go to Hotel Hilton because it's the closest." He points to

it on the map. "You will have a car waiting so when we land, you

can follow them. Do you both have everything you need?" Morrow

and Lowes nod in unison.

"Luke, I need you to study this catalog," he hands it to him,

and here is everything that you will need, and are required to have."

He goes back into his briefcase, and starts to take things out of it.

One, by one, he hands them over to Luke.

248

"This is your new passport, and driver's license. Luke looks at them and nods. "This is your cellphone and I will show you how to use it. You need to be careful with it. It has a chip in it that once you activate, the phone explodes. I would learn everything about the phone first. This phone will be used to track you, and everything that is said on it, is recorded and listened to at the headquarters."

Beckman smiles. "We all have personal phones that we use for personal use," he winks at Luke. "This is an earpiece," he hands it to him, "we each wear one of these when we are on duty. This is a watch that you put on your wrist, and when you want to say something, you talk to it, and the three of us will be able to hear you. The four of us are the only ones that are on the same channel. No one else will be able to hear us talk. So put in the ear piece, and put the watch on. Don't forget to look at all the things that the watch is capable of in the catalog. For right now, if you want to talk, just press the black button on the side of it."

Next, he stands up and tells Luke to join him in the back. Once they were in a room at the back of the plane, Beckman walks to a closet and takes out a black briefcase. "This is yours." He hands it to him. "This has all of our other gadgets inside and a laptop that looks like mine. Finally, I will need to have you change into a suit and tie." He opens a closet and in it are 5 suits, 5 dress shirts, 5 ties, and 5 pairs of shoes. "These should all be your size, and this is all yours. So change into one, and put the rest in this travel bag. There are socks, underwear, and toiletries in the bag," which he points to.

"How did you know what my size is?" Luke asks out of curiosity.

"I know everything that there is to know about you. I have been studying you for quite a while now. We have had our eye on you and have been contemplating asking if you would join us at NSA for quite some time. I know that there is a thing going on between you and Miss Parker. I am very confident in the fact that you will do your job well, even if you are personally involved with the victim and his family. Welcome aboard." He says as he leaves Luke alone in the little room.

Chapter 17

Back at the house, after talking with Cap, Baily walks into the house and finds Andrea still sitting at the breakfast table. *This is going to be a lot tougher*, she thought. She is now in charge of watching Dr. Parker. Baily doesn't seem to like her much, especially since she found out about her relationship with Luke. *Luke doesn't love me, and I will get over him soon enough, but why her? What does she have that I don't?* Baily rolls her eyes when she looks at her. She walks over to her and sits down next to her.

"How are you holding up?"

"I'm okay, just worried about Matt. The man that took him, he will kill him won't he?" Andrea asks her.

"For whatever reason that he took your brother, he needs him. He won't kill him."

Hopefully they will find him, before he does. "Prochesky is using you as insurance though, and I need to watch you at all times."

"What do you mean?"

"What I mean is that Prochesky is using your brother, and the only reason that your brother is helping him, is because Prochesky threatened your life. Prochesky is capable of a lot of things, and if your brother doesn't obey, he will go after you. There will be an officer stationed at the front entrance of the house at all times, and there will be one at the back of the house, too. Your brother never thought to secure the house?"

"No, my brother never thought about their security to my knowledge. He never imagined that he could become the object of some evil person. But his life was never in danger before, either. For what I know, I don't think he thought that his computer knowledge could get him into trouble like this. Is there anything that I can do about it?"

"Actually, I am glad you asked. I thought that we could talk about setting up a security system for the house, and you can surround the whole estate with a fence. This way, no one can get into the yard without having to pass through a front gate. I think that we could put up cameras all around the estate."

"Wow, that's a lot of work."

"Yes, it is. But with just a couple of phone calls, I can have everything done and ready to go in less than a week. It looks like it will be a necessity from now on. Do I have your permission to start on it all?"

"Yes, you do. I want my brother to feel safe when he comes home, as much as I think that he is going to hate the idea. I think that it will be best for him. I am going to go to my room now." Andrea stands up. "You can have the guest room, come on, I will show it to you." They go upstairs and Andrea gets the guest room ready. She showed her where everything was and then told her to make herself at home, while she went to her own bedroom and closed the door.

Since there were still officers present, including Cap, Baily decided to quickly go home and grab some of her things. She ran into her condo, and straight to her bedroom. She packed a few clothes, grabbed her toiletries and then with her bag, she walked out of the house. She put the bag on the passenger seat and closed the door to her car. Her cellphone rang and she answered it.

"Hello."

"Hey, it's Luke, how's it going?"

"It's going fine. I just grabbed some of my things and am on my way back to the Parker residence. Miss Parker is going to let me make some huge security adjustments to the house. So don't worry about us. We will be just fine."

"I know, when it comes to you, I don't have much to worry about. You sure know how to take care of yourself," he laughs. "We are on a flight to Paris now. We should be landing soon. I will call you if there is anything to report."

"Okay. Take care of yourself Luke," she hangs up the phone and continues the drive to the Parker house. When she pulls in, one officer is there checking ID's. He let her go in and she parked her little car in the driveway. She noticed that there were only a couple of police cars left. She walked into the house and sees Cap standing, by himself, in the living room.

"Everyone is out. There is an officer in the front, and there is one in the back. I assume that you have talked to Dr. Parker about the security measures that she will need to take?"

"Yup. I will start on the calls this morning."

"Good, I am going to get going. Our top priority from this point on is to keep the members of the Parker family safe and secure. The NSA will be in charge from here on out to apprehend Prochesky. This guy is very dangerous. I had everything checked out, and nothing on the property was found as an explosive. So for now, you are both safe." Baily walks him out.

"Have a good day, Cap."

"You too, and be careful."

Up in her room, Andrea looks out of the window. Her window overlooks the front of the house. When she saw the last police car leave, she got on her phone and dialed Luke's number.

No answer. She waited a few more minutes and decided to call him

again. She needs to know what's going on. Again, there is no

answer. She puts the phone on the nightstand and lies down

on the bed. It's 8:30 in the morning, and she needs to sleep, but

can't.

———— * ———— * ————

Luke changed into a black suit and put on a tie. He is going

to have to get used to dressing like this from now on. He looks at

himself in the mirror. He has never worn a suit on a daily basis ever

in his life. He has turned over a new leaf. He packs up the rest of the

clothes and shoes, and then takes a seat on the chair that is in the

room. He opens up the briefcase, looks in it and then closes it. He

looks at the watch. It's 8:45 am. He grabs his personal cellphone and looks at it. Two missed calls. "Shit." Andrea called him. He calls her back and she answers.

"Hello."

"Hi, how are you?"

"I'm better now since you called me. I was starting to worry about you, too."

"Sorry, I was busy, I couldn't pick up the phone. I am on my way to Paris."

"Paris? Why Paris?"

"Prochesky is taking your brother there."

"I hope you find him, before he gets killed."

"We will get him, Andie. You don't need to worry. I need to go, I will call you as soon as I can, okay?"

"Okay, be careful, I love you."

"I love you, too, Andie. Bye." The door of the room opens

and Beckman walks in.

"We will be arriving in approximately 6 hrs. I am going to

get some shut eye and I suggest that you do the same." He walks out

of the room and Luke follows him out. The other two agents were

already asleep. Luke takes his seat and slides the back down. He is

going to try to get some sleep, but he feels that he is too nervous and

excited to do so.

———— * – ———— * ————

Baily puts her clothes in the dresser that is in the guestroom

and walks into the bathroom attached to it. This is the biggest

bathroom that she has ever seen. *Wow and a king sized bed, wow, wow, wow! This place is amazing! This guestroom is as big as my whole condo.* She closes her eyes. *I can get used to this. This is going to be like a vacation for me. How bad can it be to hang out with Andrea Parker for a while. After all, Andrea has a recently widowed brother who is extremely sexy, smart, and rich, hmm.* She smiles to herself, then begins to make the phone calls to fortify the Parker estate.

Andrea feels so much better after talking with Luke. She used the bathroom and got into her bed. She knows that Luke will find him. She closed her eyes and thought about him. She thought about how much her life has changed this past week. Some things better than others. Luke proposed and that made her feel the happiest. But Matthew is in serious danger, and his life is in turmoil. She wants him to be happy and content in his life. She takes a picture off of her headboard and looks at it for a while. It was her favorite picture of her family. She remembered that day like it was yesterday.

The college graduation was at noon, and her parents were there at 10:30 am. They were so excited. She remembered her father telling her that morning, how happy he was that she graduated, and how proud he was of her. After the graduation ceremony, they went to La Chateux for dinner. Luke had his plans with his mother that day, so they met up later. Luke picked her up at her house and they went to the mountains and watched the sunset. Andrea smiles at the picture and then puts it back on the shelf. She gets comfortable, and finally falls asleep.

Chapter 18

Sitting in first class, Prochesky is alert and well aware that the NSA knows that they are on their way to Paris. He gets on his cell and dials a friend that he knows he can count on.

"Hi, Marcel, it's Eric, I need a huge favor."…. "I want to use your guesthouse for a few days."…. "Thanks will do." *Now that I have a place in mind, that the NSA doesn't know about, all I have to do is lose them on the way there. The car will be waiting for me in the parking lot when I land. I just need Mr. Parker to be able to keep up with the speed that I need him to travel.* He looks over at him, asleep. *I packed the medicine that he needs in the backpack. I need him well enough to rewrite the program. Once he's all done, I'll kill him.* He smirks. There are two agents from the NSA on the plane. He needs to figure out a way to lose them. The plane doesn't land for a number of hours, which gives him plenty of time to conjure up a

plan. Later, he gets up and goes to the bathroom. On his way back,

he decides to check out the rest of the plane. He walks up and down

the aisles, aware that the two agents are watching his every move.

He gets back to his seat and looks at his watch, time is moving

along.

_____ * _____ * _____

Luke woke up and looked at his watch. *Damn it, we still have*

an hour before we land. He looks over at the other three agents.

Morrow and Lowes are still asleep, but Beckman was going

through some papers. Luke got up and joined him.

"I can't sleep," Luke takes a seat.

"You know, when I had my first case 10 years ago, I was so set on solving it that I didn't sleep a whole week. I was obsessed." Beckman continues, "when I solved it, I took a vacation and slept all through it."

"It took you a week to solve the case?"

"No, actually, it took about three months. I was just so excited and nervous at the same time that I couldn't sleep the first week. After the first week, I only slept for a few hours a night. But that was all I needed. To this day, I still only sleep a few hours a night."

"Can I ask you something?" Beckman nods as he passes a coffee carafe and cup to Luke. "Did you ever figure out who the leak is?"

"No, not yet, but we have been monitoring two agents who I

believe could be guilty. I have one more agent that is on my team,

Jack Smith, but he isn't here with us. He is back at the

headquarters. He is my main computer guy. Whatever I need, he

finds out for me. He has been monitoring the agents, as well. I will

introduce you to him when we get back."

"Have you always worked with the same people?"

"I have worked with Agent Morrow for the last 8 years.

Agent Lowes joined the team 5 years ago, and Agent Jack Smith has

been working with me since I started ten years ago. I trust

my team and you are going to have to learn to trust us, too." Luke

nods and Beckman looks at his watch.

"Lowes, Morrow," he yells out and the two automatically sit

up in their chairs. "Showtime in fifteen."

———— * ———— * ————

He wakes up Matthew and tells him that that they will soon

land. He leans over to him and whispers into his ear, "there are two

agents following us. If you don't go exactly where I tell you to go,

and if you try anything funny, I will kill your sister."

"I understand," Matthew replies and nods. "What do I need

to do?"

"As soon as the plane lands, we will exit through that door,"

he points to an exit at the front of the plane. "There is a car waiting

for us there. I will need you to be able to walk as fast as you can, and

keep up with me."

"How do you plan to lose them?"

"Don't worry about that. I will take care of that in my own

way." The seatbelt light goes on and the pilot talks through the intercom.

"We will be landing in five minutes. Everyone to their seats, and seatbelts buckled. Keep them on until we arrive at the terminal and the seatbelt lights go off. Thank you for flying with Air France. Have a great trip."

_____ * _____ * _____

Luke's plane landed 10 minutes ago. Agents Morrow and Lowes are ready to move. There is only one exit out of the airport, and they are waiting for Prochesky and Matthew to head out. Their job is to tail them and let Beckman, who is with Luke already at the hotel, know where Prochesky is headed. Agent Morrow is behind the wheel of the black BMW sedan and Agent Lowes is in the passenger seat. They were ready to go.

Agent Lowes presses the black button on his wristwatch and says,

"We are ready to go. No sign of them yet."

"Good," Beckman replies. We just got into the hotel room. I am ready to turn on the computer so that we can get a visual. Keep your glasses on. We will be watching through your eyes." Luke stands next to him and watches with amazement.

"You will be able to catch everything on video?"

"Yes. We will watch everything that Morrow and Lowes see. We will get the car and the license plate number. Jack, who is back at the headquarters, will be watching everything, too." The computer screen turns on and Beckman types in some kind of code. The next thing that shows up on the screen, is the airport. "We have the visual.

Jack, you in?" Luke can hear everything that is being said through

his ear piece. After a couple of minutes, a black, Audi sedan, leaves

the airport.

"That's him," Agent Morrow says as he starts to follow.

They were right behind him.

Prochesky is well aware of his tail and proceeded to drive.

He is planning on losing them in Paris. He drives towards the Eifel

Tower, and with so many cars there, he has a chance of losing them.

He starts to speed up a little and watches the BMW through the

rearview mirror. He shifts left and right from lane to lane and back

again around the circle. *Damn, this guy is good.* After driving around

the Eiffel Tower a couple of times, Prochesky becomes irritated.

Time for plan B. He drives out of the city and heads towards Lyon.

He puts the car in gear and takes off, and Agent Morrow does the same. He loves France. After spending years here, he knows every road there is to know. He is getting ready to do some serious damage. He drives for twenty minutes, then Prochesky pulls over to the right side of the road and stops. As the BMW closes in, he takes his laser device from the inside pocket of his suit jacket and aims it at the left, front tire. He cackles and laughs as he activates the laser. The next thing that Luke and Beckman see is an explosion and the screen goes blank.

"Son of a bitch! Morrow, Lowes, can you hear me?" …silence… "Lowes are you there? Morrow?" Still, no reply. "Jack, we are heading out. Call the Paris police and put out an APB on Prochesky. Come on Luke, let's hurry. We lost them." They run out to their car and Beckman drives off.

After getting dressed, Andrea walks down to the kitchen and finds Officer Baily on the phone. She grabs a cup of coffee and sits down at the table. Baily gets off of the phone and comes over to her.

"I just got off the phone with a security company. The company crew will be here shortly. They will install a security alarm system and cameras around the house. Later in the afternoon, a contracting company will be here. The contractor will show you a plan and you will need to approve it and sign the paperwork for that as well."

"You sure don't like to waste any time," Andrea comments.

"No, no I don't," Baily takes a sip of her coffee and smiles at

Andrea, "you better eat something."

"Yes, I will make us both something. Have you talked with

Luke yet?"

"No, I haven't, I'm sure that he will call when he has news. It

is best not to call and bother him." Baily replied, as the doorbell

rang. "That must be the security company. They are right on time. I

will show them in."

_____ * _____ * _____

When they pull up to the scene of the accident, Luke and

Beckman run over to the flipped car. A rescue team has already

pulled Lowes and Morrow out of the vehicle. They are both dead.

"That crazy son of a bitch!" Beckman hollers as Luke, upset

himself, stands by him. Saddened and frustrated by the demise of two of his most accomplished and trusted agents, Beckman decides to contact Interpol. Beckman knows that although NSA is far-reaching and has extended its tentacles of espionage worldwide, now on European soil, NSA is not involved with foreign spies as he had hoped them to be by this time. He contacts an Interpol inspector with whom he has crossed paths with over the years, Inspector Pierre Virant. Inspector Virant would know more of Prochesky's contacts and acquaintances in France.

"Luke, this was to be a watch and learn trip for you, but due to the loss of my two agents, you will be playing a more active role and will be more involved than I had planned for you. You will be coming with me to meet my Interpol connection. I will do all of the talking, so don't say anything unless you are directly requested to do so. The way we operate in the US as an agent of NSA is very different than here in France. There is a respect and protocol that we must abide by. I am as anxious as you are to get Prochesky. I know that you want to get Mr. Parker home safely as fast as possible, but I need to get Prochesky. I want him to pay for the lives of the people that he has killed, especially my two agents."

"Okay, Beckman, I will come along and do what you ask of me. But know that I will have a tough time keeping my mouth shut."

They meet up in a café outside of Paris, in Boulogne-Billancourt, southwest of Paris along the River Seine.

"Good day, Mr. Beckman. Who is this whom you have brought to our meeting? I was not aware you were bringing someone," Inspector Virant says in a thick accent.

"This is an agent new to the Prochesky case, Agent Kith. He

is new to the ways of Interpol and will be learning all that he can, as we work together to try and capture Prochesky."

Inspector Virant queries the fact that NSA is in need of his assistance,

"We have been monitoring the communications NSA has been engaged in with a number of foreign agents, among them Prochesky."

Embarrassed by this being brought to light, Beckman must, in a diplomatic way, ask Inspector Virant, to give him all of the information that he has. Beckman needs to know who at NSA has had contact with Prochesky.

"Like the many aliases and passports they own, spies have multiple cell phones to use for communication. Different countries use different bands and networks on different continents.

Can you help us out, Inspector Virant?"

"Prochesky is most likely using a European based cell phone. We will delve into our information and see who Prochesky has been in touch with the last couple of months. He has a few contacts in the Paris region. Many of them have chateaus or villas. Maybe one of the contacts lent him a place to hide out."

"Can you inform me as to whom Prochesky has been in contact with at the NSA? I am aware that we have a leak, a mole within our organization. I have not been able to pinpoint exactly who it is."

"Yes, I can do that for you. We must band together to keep the world safe."

They finish their coffees and part their ways. Inspector Virant has promised to give Beckman a call, as soon as he attains the information.

"I don't think that I like all of this waiting around. Don't you think that we should just go out there and look for him?" Luke questions Beckman as they sit in the hotel lobby and drink another café au lait.

"Things operate here in a different manner. Just because we are sitting around and waiting, doesn't mean that things are not rolling along. You have to remember that we are on foreign soil. We can't take full jurisdiction here. Interpol and the French police are in charge, and we are going to need all of the help we can get to apprehend Prochesky. What we need now is some rest. I will get you as soon as I hear anything. I am going up to my room."

At 3:00 pm, Beckman received the phone call that he has been waiting for. He has learned who the leak is and called up Jack

Smith, only to find out the mole took a leave of absence yesterday morning. *Great, I am sure that he is on his way to meet up with Prochesky. We will be able to nail them both at the same time.* After talking with Inspector Virant, they were able to come up with a plan to catch Prochesky. Inspector Virant told Beckman of a call made hours ago between Prochesky and a Paris acquaintance who has an estate nearby. They said that they would meet up at the guesthouse where they think that Prochesky is staying at in one hour. Beckman went to Luke's room and woke him. He told him that they will be meeting up with Inspector Virant and the police, a quarter of a mile away from the estate. Beckman's phone rings and he answers,

"Yeah".... "Thanks, Jack, I will get right back to you." He hangs up and turns to Luke.

"We have another problem. Jack just informed me that

279

Prochesky made a call to the US today and it wasn't to the mole. It

was to an officer that works with you. The last name is Baily."

"Shit." Luke interrupts, "she is in charge of watching Andrea.

She is staying with her until we get Prochesky and Matt."

"You give a call to the both of them. Make sure you warn

Andrea. I will call Jack back and make sure that he informs Captain

Corrigan of Baily's relationship with Prochesky and that Andrea's

safety must be secured. We can make all the calls on the way to the

estate."

They pack up what they need and head out. Beckman spoke

with Jack but Luke wasn't able to get a hold of Andrea or Baily. His

mind starts to wander as he hopes that Andrea is safe. He wondered

if Baily would hurt Andrea just because of the way she feels towards

him. Luke's adrenaline is pumping as they are on the road.

"Remember, Luke, we are here to follow, not lead, and be careful," Beckman said as he parked the car behind a French squad car. They meet up with Inspector Virant who was talking, in French, with some of the men.

"Aah, Agent Beckman, Agent Kith, thank you for joining us," Inspector Virant greets them. "We are ready to go now," he says in his mouth piece as all of the officers start to move in on the guesthouse. Beckman and Luke followed behind. There was only one light on and there were two shadows that were seen through the draped covered window in the front. The officers worked fast shooting smoke bombs through the window. Entering the guesthouse, they spotted Prochesky with a gun aimed at Agent Pat Patton. Within seconds, Prochesky began his shooting rampage by hitting Pat Patton. He swung his gun toward anyone he could see through the smoke shooting wildly. Prochesky throws a table on its side and takes cover. Luke hits the floor using the smoke to his advantage and crawls around behind Prochesky. He shoots and wings Prochesky in his firing arm shoulder.

"He's down," Luke yells out, "Stop shooting!" Inspector Virant gets on a loud speaker and says,

"Cease fire! Cease fire! Prochesky is down!" As the noise ceases and the smoke clears, it is apparent that a number of people have been struck by Prochesky. Inspector Virant and Beckman approached Luke holding Prochesky under guard. Luke tells Beckman,

"He's all yours. I am searching for Matt."

A few minutes later, Luke came over to Beckman who was still discussing things over with Inspector Virant and interrupted them.

"I can't find Matt anywhere. I searched the whole premise and there is no sign of him anywhere."

Inspector Virant informs him that there is a tunnel connecting the guesthouse to the main house. "There has to be a trap door that leads to the tunnel. Let us all start looking. Mr. Parker has to be on the premises or nearby."

Chapter 19

It's 6:00 pm, the workmen have left, and hunger finally takes over Andrea. She has been busy all day discussing the aspects of the security assessments with Baily and the workers.

"Baily, are you as hungry as I am? I haven't eaten anything besides eggs and a bagel in the morning. I am going to search the freezer and see if I can whip us up something to eat."

"That would be great," Baily replies as she watches Andrea rummage through the freezer. *Eric called me today and told me to make Andrea suffer a little so that he could get a video going for Matthew. I am so glad that I hooked up with him a few nights ago. We made a deal to meet up in Mexico after all of this is over. We are going to be billionaires soon, and I can't wait! Now is the perfect opportunity to grab her.* Baily grabs a knife from the knife block and sneaks up on Andrea from behind. She grabs her around the neck and Andrea screams.

"Do what I say and I won't hurt you," Baily says to her and Andrea nods. Baily releases her, and Andrea, holding a piece of frozen meat, turns around and hits Baily on the head with it. Surprised by the blow, Baily staggers back a couple of steps but manages not to fall. She lunges toward Andrea with the knife still in hand. Andrea deflects the knife with a pan from the counter and they become engaged in a wrestling match. They fall on the floor and Andrea holds on to Baily's wrist as Baily tries to stab her. They wrestle and grapple on the floor between the island and cabinets. Andrea, familiar with the kitchen, slips her hand into a cupboard and pulls out a small, cast iron skillet. She aims for Baily's head and with a glancing blow, stuns Baily as Captain Corrigan walks in. Cap

lunges for Baily pulling her to her feet and cuffs her. Other officers

come in and take Baily away and Cap helps Andrea to her feet.

"Are you okay? Do I need to call the paramedics?" Cap asks

her as she straightens herself.

"No, I am okay. I sure didn't see this coming," Andrea

shakes her head.

"I have been in contact with Agent Beckman. He had called

to tell me that Prochesky has been in contact with Officer Baily.

They will also hopefully apprehend Prochesky in short order.

I will keep you company until we hear some news."

———— * ———— * ————

At the front of the guesthouse under a window a locked trap door is found. Luke breaks the hasp, lifts the door and sees a dark hole. He asks for a flashlight and one is passed to him. He hurries down the stairs and finds Matt bound and gagged twenty feet away from the entrance of the tunnel.

"Matt can you hear me?" Luke says as he removes the gag.

"Luke," he mumbles, "I, I, I'm so tired." Matt responds as Luke unbinds his hands and feet. Luke lifts him up and half carries him up the steps, out of the guesthouse and to a waiting ambulance. Inspector Virant tells Luke and Beckman that Matt will be taken to a local hospital. Beckman tells Luke to go ahead and ride along and that he will meet him at the hospital as soon as he finishes

287

everything here.

Inspector Virant and Beckman survey the damage at the guesthouse. Three French officers have been wounded, as well as, Prochesky, who is being transferred to a prison hospital for treatment. Pat Patton, who was killed, will be shipped back to the United States along with the bodies of Morrow and Lowes.

At the hospital, after assessment, it has been determined that Matthew has contracted an infection in his wound. The doctors have determined that he will have to remain hospitalized for a few days for an infusion of intravenous antibiotics before he is able to return to the States. Beckman joins Luke at the hospital to bring him up to date on the case. He tells Luke that he can stay and accompany Mr. Parker back to the States when he is released from the doctor's care.

"I will be traveling back with the bodies of Morrow, Lowes,

and Patton. Contact me when Matthew gets released. I will have a private jet ready for you to fly home on. Have you been in contact with Andrea?" Beckman inquires.

"Yes, I have talked with Andrea. Officer Baily has been arrested and Andrea is safe. Matthew will be fine, too."

"You did really well, Luke. I hope I see you back at NSA soon."

"You will see me, for sure," Luke replies as he shakes Beckman's hand.

Chapter 20

Five days have passed, and Andrea waits at home for Matt

and Luke's arrival. She has spent the last couple of days cleaning

and getting the house in order. She has hired a maid and all of the

security adjustments have been taken care of. She takes the pork loin

out of the oven and checks it.

"Just a few more minutes," she says to Bella with a huge s

mile on her face. Bella, after speaking with Andrea a few days ago,

has agreed to visit with Andrea and Matthew. Andrea couldn't be

happier with the arrangement.

"I am so happy that you are here," Andrea hugs Bella again.

"I am glad, too," Bella replied as the intercom beeped.

"That must be them," Andrea looks at the TV screen in the

kitchen that showed the entrance to the driveway. She pressed a

button that opened up the gate, and together with Bella,

went outside the front door. As Luke parked the car, Andrea ran to

the passenger side and helped Matthew from the car. She carefully

hugged him and kissed him on the cheek. He wiped off the

tear that was flowing down her cheek, smiled, and said,

"I'm fine. What's with all of the security?'

"I thought that it was necessary for you to have. I am not

taking any more chances. I hope that you aren't too upset about it."

"I am okay with it," Matthew replies, but it is going to take

me a while to get used to it. I am going to slowly go in, someone else

is just as excited to see you as I am," he winks as he lets go of her

and she walks to the back of the car where Luke was getting the

luggage out of the trunk. He closes the trunk and turns to see

Andrea's beautiful, smiling face.

"Hi," he says to her as he pulls her into his arms.

"Hi," she replied and he kissed her.

Made in the USA
Lexington, KY
21 February 2015